Kate Douglas Smith Wiggin

Timothy's quest; a story for anybody, young or old, who cares to

read it

Kate Douglas Smith Wiggin

Timothy's quest; a story for anybody, young or old, who cares to read it

ISBN/EAN: 9783337057336

Printed in Europe, USA, Canada, Australia, Japan

Cover: Foto ©Andreas Hilbeck / pixelio.de

More available books at **www.hansebooks.com**

Timothy's Quest

A Story for Anybody, Young or Old
Who Cares to Read It
By Kate Douglas Wiggin
With Illustrations by
Oliver Herford

Boston and New York
Houghton, Mifflin and Company
The Riverside Press, Cambridge
M DCCC XCV

The Riverside Press, Cambridge, Mass., U.S.A.
Electrotyped and Printed by H. O. Houghton & Co.

To
Nora:
Dearest Sister,—
Sternest Critic,
Best Friend

—

CONTENTS

TIMOTHY'S QUEST

SCENE I

NUMBER THREE, MINERVA COURT
FIRST FLOOR FRONT

*Flossy Morrison learns the Secret of Death without
ever having learned the Secret of Life*

INERVA COURT! Veil thy face, O Goddess of Wisdom, for never surely was thy fair name so ill bestowed as when it was applied to this most dreary place!

It was a little less than street, a little more than alley, and its only possible claim to decency came from comparison with the busier thoroughfare out of which it opened. This was so much fouler, with its dirt and noise, its stands of refuse fruit and vegetables, its dingy shops and all the miserable traffic that the place engendered, its rickety doorways blocked with lounging men, its Blowsabellas leaning on the window-sills, that the Court seemed by contrast a most desirable and retired place of residence.

Nevertheless it was a dismal spot, with not even an air of faded gentility to recommend it. It seemed to have no better days behind it, nor to hold within itself the possibility of any future improvement.   It was narrow, and extended only the length of a city block, yet it was by no means wanting in many of the luxuries which mark this era of modern civilization.   At each corner there were groceries, with commodious sample-rooms attached, and a small saloon, called "The Dearest Spot" (which it undoubtedly was in more senses than one), in the basement of a house at the farther end. It was necessary, however, for the bibulous native who dwelt in the middle of the block to waste some valuable minutes in dragging himself to one of these fountains of bliss at either end; but at the time my story opens a wide-awake philanthropist was fitting up a neat and attractive little barroom, called "The Oasis," at a point equally distant between the other two springs of human joy.

This benefactor of humanity had a vaulting ambition.   He desired to slake the thirst of every man in Christendom ; but as this was impossible from the very nature of things, he determined to settle in some arid spot like Minerva Court, and irrigate

it so sweetly and copiously that all men's
noses would blossom as the roses. To supply his brothers' wants, and create new ones
at the same time, was his purpose in estab-
lishing this Oasis in the Desert of Minerva
Court; and it might as well be stated here
that he was prospered in his undertaking,
as any man is sure to be who cherishes
lofty ideals and attends to his business in-
dustriously.

The Minerva Courtier thus had good
reason to hope that the supply of liquid re-
freshment would bear some relation to the
demand, and that the march of modern pro-
gress would continue to diminish the distance between his own mouth and that of
the bottle, which, as he took it, was the
be-all and end-all of existence.

At present, however, as the Oasis was
not open to the public, children carrying
pitchers of beer were often to be seen hurrying to and fro on their miserable errands.
There were very few children in Minerva
Court, thank God! — they were not popular
there. There were frowzy, sleepy-looking
women hanging out of their windows, gos-

siping with their equally unkempt and hag-
gard neighbors ; apathetic men sitting on the
doorsteps, in their shirt - sleeves, smoking ;
a dull, dirty baby or two disporting itself in
the gutter ; while the sound of a melancholy
accordion floated from an upper chamber,
and added its discordant mite to the general
desolation.

The sidewalks had apparently never known
the touch of a broom, and the middle of the
street looked more like an elongated junk-
heap than anything else.   Every evil smell
known to the nostrils of man was abroad in
the air, and several were floating about waiting modestly to be classified, after which
they intended to come to the front and outdo
the others if they could.

That was Minerva Court !   A little piece
of your world, my world, God's world (and
the Devil's), lying peacefully fallow, awaiting the services of some inspired Home
Missionary Society.

In a front room of Number Three, a dilap-
idated house next the corner, there lay a
still, white shape, with two women watching
by it.

A sheet covered it. Candles burned at the head, striving to throw a gleam of light on a dead face that for many a year had never been illuminated from within by the brightness of self-forgetting love or kindly sympathy. If you had raised the sheet, you would have seen no happy smile as of a half-remembered, innocent childhood; the smile — is it of peaceful memory or serene anticipation? — that sometimes shines on the faces of the dead.

Innocent Childhood

Such life-secrets as were exposed by Death and written on that still countenance in characters that all might read, were painful ones. Flossy Morrison was dead. The name "Flossy" was a relic of what she termed her better days (Heaven save the mark!), for she had been called Mrs. Morrison of late years, — " Mrs. F. Morrison," who took " children to board, and no questions asked " — nor answered. She had lived forty-five years, as men reckon summers and winters ; but she had never learned, in all that time, to know her Mother, Nature, her Father, God, nor her brothers and sisters, the children of the world. She had lived friendless and unfriendly, keeping none of the ten commandments, nor yet the eleventh, which is the greatest of all ; and now there was no human being to slip a flower into the still hand, to kiss the clay-cold lips at the remembrance of some sweet word that had fallen from them, or drop a tear and say, " I loved her ! "

Apparently, the two watchers did not regard Flossy Morrison even in the light of " the dear remains," as they are sometimes called at country funerals. They were in the best of spirits (there was an abundance of beer), and their gruesome task would be over in a few hours, for it was nearly four o'clock in the morning and the body was to be taken away at ten.

"I tell you one thing, Ettie, Flossy has n't left any bother for her friends," remarked Mrs. Nancy Simmons, settling herself back in her rocking-chair. "As she did n't own anything but the clothes on her back, there won't be any quarreling over the property!" and she chuckled at her delicate humor.

"No," answered her companion, who, whatever her sponsors in baptism had christened her, called herself Ethel Montmorency. "I s'pose the furniture, poor as it is, will pay the funeral expenses, and if she's got any debts, why, folks will have to whistle for their money, that's all."

"The only thing that worries me is the children," said Mrs. Simmons.

"You must be hard up for something to worry about, to take those young ones on your mind. They ain't yours nor mine, and what's more, nobody knows who they do belong to, and nobody cares; soon as breakfast's over we'll pack 'em off to some institution or other, and that'll be the end of it. What did Flossy say about 'em, when you spoke to her yesterday?"

"I asked her what she wanted done with

the young ones, and she said, ' Do what you like with 'em, drat 'em, — it don't make no odds to me!' and then she turned over and died. Those was the last words she spoke, dear soul ; but, Lor', she was n't more 'n half sober, and had n't been for a week."

"She was sober enough to keep her own counsel, I can tell you that," said the gentle Ethel. "I don't believe there's a living soul that knows where those children came from ; — not that anybody cares, now that there ain't any money in 'em."

"Well, as for that, I only know that when Flossy was seeing better days and lived in the upper part of the city, she used to have money come every month for taking care of the boy. Where it come from I don't know ; but I kind of surmise it was a long distance off. Then she took to drinking, and got lower and lower down until she came here, six months ago. I don't suppose the boy's folks, or whoever it was sent the money, knew the way she was living, though they could n't have cared much, for they never came to see how things were ; he was in an asylum before Flossy took him, I found that

out ; but, anyhow, the money stopped coming more than three months ago.   Flossy
wrote twice to the folks, whoever they were,
but did n't get no answer to her letters ; and
she told me that she should
turn the boy out in a week or
two if some cash did n't turn
up in that time ; she would n't
have kept him so long as this
if he had n't been so handy
taking care of the baby."

"Well, who does the baby
belong to ?"

"You ask me too much,"
replied Nancy, taking another
deep draught from the pitcher.

" So handy "

— "Help yourself, Ettie, there's plenty
more where that came from. — Flossy never
liked the boy, and always wanted to get rid
of him, but could n't afford to.   He 's a
dreadful queer, old-fashioned little kid, and
so smart that he 's gettin' to be a reg'lar
nuisance round the house.   But you see
he and the baby, — Gabrielle 's her name,
though they call her Lady Gay, or some such
trash, after that actress that comes here so

much, — well, they are so in love with one
another that wild horses could n't drag 'em
apart ; and I think Flossy had a kind of a
likin' for Gay, as much as she ever had for
anything.   I guess she never abused either
of 'em ; she was too careless for that.   And
so — what was I talkin' about ? — Oh, yes,
— I don't know who the baby is, nor who
paid for her keep, but she 's goin' to be one
o' your high-steppers, and no mistake.   She
might be Queen Victory's daughter by the
airs she puts on ; I 'd like to keep her myself if she was a little older, and I was n't
goin' away from here."

"I s'pose they 'll make an awful row at
being separated, won't they ?" asked the
younger woman.

"Oh, like as not ; but they 'll have to
have their row and get over it," said Mrs.
Simmons easily.   "You can take Timothy
to the Orphan Asylum first, and then come
back, and I 'll carry the baby to the Home
of the Ladies' Relief and Protection Society ; and if they yell they can yell, and
take it out in yellin' ; they won't get the
best of Nancy Simmons."

"Don't talk so loud, Nancy, for mercy's sake; if the boy hears you, he'll begin to take on, and we shan't get a wink of sleep. Don't let 'em know what you're goin' to do with 'em till the last minute, or you'll have trouble as sure as we sit here."

"Oh, they are sound asleep," responded Mrs. Simmons, with an uneasy look at the half-open door. "I went in and dragged a pillow out from under Timothy's head, and he never budged. He was sleepin' like a log, and so was Gay. Now, shut up, Et, and let me get three winks myself. You take the lounge, and I'll stretch out in two chairs. Wake me up at eight o'clock, if I don't wake myself; for I am clean tired out with all this fussin' and plannin', and I feel stupid enough to sleep till kingdom come."

SCENE 11

NUMBER THREE, MINERVA COURT
FIRST FLOOR BACK

*Little Timothy Jessup assumes Parental
Responsibilities*

WHEN the snores of the two watchers fell on the stillness of the death-chamber, with that cheerful regularity that betokens the sleep of the truly good, a little figure crept out of the bed in the adjoining room, and closing the door noiselessly, but with trembling fingers, stole to the window to look out at the dirty street and the gray sky, over which the first faint streaks of dawn were beginning to creep.

It was little Timothy Jessup (God alone knows whether he had any right to that special patronymic), but not the very same Tim Jessup who had kissed the baby Gay in her crib, and gone to sleep on his own hard bed in that room, a few hours before. As he stood shivering at the window, one thin hand hard pressed upon his heart to still its beating, there was a light of sudden resolve in his eyes, a new-born look of anxiety on his unchildlike face.

"I will not have Gay protectioned and reliefed, and I will not be taken away from her and sent to a 'sylum, where I can never find her again!" and with these defiant words trembling, half spoken, on his lips, he glanced from the unconscious form in the crib to the terrible door, which might open at any moment and divide him from his heart's delight, his darling, his treasure, his only joy, his own, own baby Gay.

What should he do? Run away; that was the only solution of the matter, and no very difficult one either. The cruel women were asleep; the awful Thing that had been Flossy would never speak again; and no one else in Minerva Court cared enough for them to pursue them very far or very long.

"And so," thought Timothy swiftly, "I will get things ready, take Gay, and steal softly out of the back door, and run away to the 'truly' country, where none of these bad people ever can find us, and where I can get a mother for Gay; somebody to 'dopt her and love her till I grow up a man and take her to live with me."

The moment this thought darted into

Timothy's mind, it began to shape itself in definite action.

Gabrielle, or Lady Gay, as Flossy called her, in honor of her favorite stage heroine, had been tumbled into her crib half dressed the night before. The only vehicle kept for her use in the family stables was a clothes-basket, mounted on four wooden wheels and cushioned with a dingy shawl. A yard of clothes-line was tied on to one end, and in this humble conveyance the Princess would have to be trans-ported from the Ogre's castle, for she was scarcely old enough to accompany the Prince on foot, even if he had dared to risk de-tection by waking her ; so the clothes-basket must be

"*A shabby suit of clothes*"

her chariot, and Timothy her charioteer, as on many a less fateful expedition.

After he had changed his ragged night-gown for a shabby suit of clothes, he took Gay's one clean apron out of a rickety

bureau drawer ("for I can never find a mother for her if she's too dirty," he thought),
her Sunday hat from the same receptacle,
and last of all a comb, and a faded Japanese
parasol that stood in a corner. These he
deposited under the old shawl that decorated
the floor of the chariot. He next groped
his way in the dim light toward a mantel-
shelf, and took down a savings-bank, — a
florid little structure with "Bank of England" stamped over the miniature door, into
which the jovial gentleman who frequented
the house often slipped pieces of silver for
the children, and into which Flossy dipped
only when she was in a state of temporary
financial embarrassment. Timothy did not
dare to jingle it ; he could only hope that as
Flossy had not been in her usual health of
late (though in more than her usual "spirits"), she had not felt obliged to break the
bank.

Now for provisions. There were plenty
of "funeral baked meats" in the kitchen;
so he hastily gathered a dozen cookies into a
towel and stowed them in the coach with the
other sinews of war.

So far, well and good ; but the worst was
to come. With his heart beating in his
bosom like a trip-hammer, and his eyes di-
lated with fear, he stepped to the door between the two rooms, and opened it softly.
Two thundering snores, pitched in such different keys that they must have proceeded
from two separate sets of nasal organs, reas-
sured the boy.   He looked out into the alley.
"Not a creature was stirring, not even a
mouse."   The Minerva Courtiers could not
be owls as well as hawks, and there was not
even the ghost of a sound to be heard.   Satisfied that all was well, Timothy went back
to the bedroom, and lifted the battered
clothes-basket, trucks and all, in his slender
arms, carried it up the alley and down the
street a little distance, and deposited it on
the pavement beside a vacant plot of ground.
This done, he sped back to the house.
"How beautifully they snore !" he thought,
as he stood again on the threshold. "Shall I
leave 'em a letter ? . . . P"raps I better . . .
and then they won't follow us and bring us
back." So he scribbled a line on a bit of torn
paper bag, and pinned it on the enemies'
door.

" A kind Lady is goin to Adopt
us it is a Grate ways off so do not
Hunt good by.   TIM."

Now all was ready. No; one thing more.
Timothy had been met in the street by a
pretty young girl a few weeks before. The
love of God was smiling in her heart, the
love of children shining in her eyes; and
she led him, a willing captive, into a mis-
sion Sunday-school near by. So much in
earnest was the sweet little teacher, and so
hungry for any sort of good tidings was the
starved little pupil, that Timothy "got religion" then and there, as simply and nat-
urally as a child takes its mother's milk.
He was probably in a state of crass igno-
rance regarding the Thirty-nine Articles ; but
it was the "engrafted word," of which the
Bible speaks, that had blossomed in Timothy's heart ; the living seed had always been
there, waiting for some beneficent fostering
influence; for he was what dear Charles
Lamb would have called a natural "king-
dom-of-heavenite." Thinking, therefore, of

Miss Dora's injunction to pray over all the
extraordinary affairs of life and as many of
the ordinary ones as possible, he hung his
tattered straw hat on the bed-post, and knelt
beside Gay's crib with this whispered
prayer : —

"*Our Father who art in heaven, please
help me to find a mother for Gay, the kind
that she can call Mamma, and another one for
me, if there's enough, but not unless. Please
excuse me for taking away the clothes-basket,
which does not exactly belong to us ; but if I
do not take it, dear heavenly Father, how will
I get Gay to the railroad? And
if I don't take the Japanese umbrella she will get freckled and
nobody will adopt her on account
of her red hair. No more at
present, as I am in a great hurry.
Amen.*"

He put on his hat, stooped
over the sleeping baby, and took
her in his faithful arms, — arms
that had never failed her yet.
She half opened her eyes, and
seeing that she was safe on her

*Safe on Timothy's
Shoulder*

beloved Timothy's shoulder, clasped her dimpled arms tight about his neck, and with a
long sigh drifted off again into the land of
dreams.   Bending beneath her weight, he
stepped for the last time across the threshold,
not even daring to close the door behind him.

Up the alley and round the corner he
sped, as fast as his trembling legs could
carry him.   Just as he was within sight of
the goal of his ambition, that is, the chariot
aforesaid, he fancied he heard the sound of
hurrying feet behind him.   To his fevered
imagination the tread was like that of an
avenging army on the track of the foe.   He
did not dare to look behind.   On ! for the
clothes-basket and liberty !   He would re-
linquish the Japanese umbrella, the cookies,
the comb, and the apron, — all the booty, in
fact, — as an inducement for the enemy to
retreat, but he would never give up the pris-
oner.

On the feet hurried, faster and faster.
He stooped to put Gay in the basket, and
turned in despair to meet his pursuers,
when a little, grimy, rough-coated, lop-eared,
split-tailed thing, like an animated rag-bag,

leaped upon his knees; whimpering with joy, and imploring, with every grace that his simple doggish heart could suggest, to be one of the eloping party.

Rags had followed them!

Timothy was so glad to find it no worse that he wasted a moment in embracing the dog, whose delirious joy at the prospect of this probably dinnerless and supperless expedition was ludicrously exaggerated. Then he took up the rope and trundled the chariot gently down a side street leading to the station.

Everything worked to a charm. They met only an occasional milk (and water) man, starting on his matutinal rounds, for it was now after four o'clock, and one or two cavaliers of uncertain gait, just returning to their homes, several hours too late for their own good; but these gentlemen were in no condition of mind to be over-interested, and the little fugitives were troubled with no questions as to their intentions.

Thus they went out into the world together, these three: Timothy Jessup (if it was Jessup), brave little knight, nameless nobleman, tracing his descent back to God, the Father of us all, and bearing the Divine likeness more than most of us; the little Lady Gay, — somebody — nobody — any-body, — from nobody knows where, — destination equally uncertain; and Rags, of pedigree most doubtful, scutcheon quite obscured by blots, but a perfect gentleman, true-hearted and loyal to the core, — in fact, an angel in fur. These three, with the clothes-basket as personal property and a toy Bank of England as security, went out to seek their fortune; and, unlike Lot's wife, without daring to look behind, shook the dust of Minerva Court from off their feet forever and forever.

SCENE III

THE RAILWAY STATION

Timothy plans a Campaign, and Providence assists materially in carrying it out, or vice versa

B Y dint of skillful generalship, Timothy gathered his forces on a green bank just behind the railway depot, cleared away a sufficient number of tin cans and oyster-shells to make a flat space for the chariot of war, which had now become simply a cradle, and sat down, with Rags curled up at his feet, to plan the campaign.

He pushed back the ragged hat from his waving hair, and, clasping his knees with his hands, gazed thoughtfully at the towering chimneys in the foreground and the white-winged ships in the distant harbor. There was a glimpse of something like a man's purpose in the sober eyes; and as the morning

sunlight fell upon his earnest face, the angel
in him came to the surface, and crowded the
"boy part" quite out of sight, as it has a
way of doing sometimes with children.

How some father - heart would have
throbbed with pride to own him, and how
gladly lifted the too heavy burden from his
childish shoulders!

Timothy Jessup, aged ten or eleven, or
thereabouts, — the records had not been kept

Timothy surveying the Situation

with absolute exactness, — Timothy Jessup,
somewhat ragged, all forlorn, and none too
clean at the present moment, was a poet,
philosopher, and lover of the beautiful. The
dwellers in Minerva Court had never discov-
ered the fact; for, although he had lived in
that world, he had most emphatically never

been of it. He was a boy of strange notions, and the vocabulary in which he expressed them was stranger still; furthermore, he had gentle manners, which must have been indigenous, as they had certainly never been cultivated; and, although he had been in the way of handling pitch for many a day, it had been powerless to defile him, such was the essential purity of his nature.

To find a home and a mother for Lady Gay had been Timothy's secret longing ever since he had heard people say that Flossy Morrison might die. He had once enjoyed all the comforts of a Home with a capital H; but it was the cosy one with the little "h" that he so much desired for her.

Not that he had any ill treatment to remember in the excellent institution of which he was for several years an inmate. The matron was an amiable and hard-working woman, who wished to do her duty to all the children under her care; but it would be an inspired human being indeed who could give a hundred and fifty motherless or fatherless children all the education and care and training they needed, to say nothing of the love

that they missed and craved.   What wonder,
then, that an occasional hungry little soul
starved for want of something not provided
by the management ; say, a morning cuddle
in mother's bed or a ride on father's knee, —
in short, the sweet daily jumble of lap-
trotting, gentle caressing, endearing words,
twilight stories, motherly tucks-in-bed, good-
night kisses, — all the dear, simple, every-
day accompaniments of the home with the
little " h."

Timothy Jessup, bred in such an atmos-
phere, would have gladdened every life that
touched his at any point.   Plenty of wistful
men and women would have thanked God
nightly on their knees for the gift of such a
son ; and here he was, sitting on a tin can,
bowed down with family cares, while thou-
sands of graceless little scalawags were slap-
ping the faces of their French nurse-maids
and bullying their parents, in that very city.
— Ah me !

As for the tiny Lady Gay, she had all the
winsome virtues to recommend her.   No one
ever feared that she would die young out of
sheer goodness.   You would not have loved

her so much for what she was as because
you could not help yourself. This feat once
accomplished, she blossomed into a thousand
graces, each one more bewitching than the
last you noted.

Where, in the name of all the sacred laws
of heredity, did the child get her sunshiny
nature? Born in misery, and probably in
sin, nurtured in wretchedness and poverty,
she had brought her "radiant morning visions" with her into the world. Like
Wordsworth's immortal babe, "with trailing
clouds of glory" had she come, from God
who was her home; and the heaven that lies
about us all in our infancy, — that Garden
of Eden into which we are all born, like
the first man and the first woman, — that
heaven lay about her still, stronger than the
touch of earth.

What if the room were desolate and bare?
The yellow sunbeams stole through the narrow window, and in the shaft of light they
threw across the dirty floor Gay played, —
oblivious of everything save the flickering
golden rays that surrounded her.

The raindrops chasing each other down

the dingy pane, the snowflakes melting softly
on the casement, the brown leaf that the
wind blew into her lap as she sat on the
sidewalk, the chirp of the little beggar-spar-
rows over the cobblestones, all these brought
as eager a light into her baby eyes as the
costliest toy.   With no earthly father or
mother to care for her, she seemed to be
God's very own baby, and He amused her
in his own good way; first by locking her
happiness within her own soul (the only
place where it is ever safe for a single moment), and then by putting her under Timothy's paternal ministrations.

Timothy's mind traveled back over the
past, as he sat among the tin cans and looked
at Rags and Gay.   It was a very small story,
if he ever found any one who would care
to hear it.   There was a long journey in a
great ship, a wearisome illness of many
weeks, — or was it months? — when his
curls had been cut off, and all his memories
with them ; then there was the Home ; then
there was Flossy, who came to take him
away ; then — oh, bright, bright spot! oh,
blessed time! — there was baby Gay ; then,

worse than all, there was Minerva Court. But he did not give many minutes to reminiscence. He first broke open the Bank of England, and threw it away, after finding to his joy that their fortune amounted to one dollar and eighty-five cents. This was so much in advance of his expectations that he laughed aloud, and Rags, wagging his tail with such vigor that he nearly broke it in two, jumped into the cradle and woke the baby.

Then there was a happy family circle, you may believe me, and with good reason, too! A trip to the country (meals and lodging uncertain, but that was a trifle), a sight of green meadows, where Timothy would hear real birds sing in the trees, and Gay would gather wild-flowers, and Rags would chase, and perhaps — who knows? — catch, toothsome squirrels and fat little field-mice, of which the country dogs visiting Minerva Court had told the most mouth-watering tales. Gay's transport knew no bounds. Her child-heart felt no regret for the past, no care for the present, no anxiety for the future. The only world she cared for was

in her sight ; and she had never, in her brief
experience, gazed upon it with more radiant
anticipation than on this sunny June morning, when she had opened her bright eyes on
a pleasant, odorous bank of oyster-shells, instead of on the accustomed surroundings of
Minerva Court.

Breakfast was first in order.

There was a pump conveniently near, and
the oyster-shells made capital cups. Gay
had three cookies, Timothy two, and Rags
one ; but there was no statute of limitations
placed on the water ; every one had as much
as he could drink.

The little matter of toilets came next.
Timothy took the dingy rag which did duty
for a handkerchief, and, calling the pump
again into requisition, scrubbed Gay's face
and hands tenderly, but firmly. Her clothes
were then all smoothed down tidily, but the
clean apron was kept for the eventful moment when her future mother should first
be allowed to behold the form of her adopted
child.

The comb was then brought out, and her
mop of red-gold hair was assisted to fall in

wet spirals all over her lovely head. Her
Sunday hat being tied on, as the crowning
glory, this lucky little princess, this child of
Fortune, so inestimably rich in her own
opinion, this daughter of the gods, I say, was
returned to the basket, where she endeavored
to keep quiet until the next piece of delight-
ful unexpectedness should rise from fairy-
land upon her excited gaze.

Timothy and Rags now went to the pump,
and Rags was held under the spout. This
was a new and bitter experience, and he
wished for a few brief moments that he had
never joined the noble army of deserters,
but had stayed where dirt was fashionable.
Being released, the sense of abnormal clean-
liness mounted to his brain, and he tore
breathlessly round in a circle seventy-seven
times without stopping. This only dried his
hair and amused Gay, who was beginning
to find the basket confining, and who clamored for "Timfy" to take her to "yide."
Timothy attended to himself last, as usual.
He put his own head under the pump, and
scrubbed his face and hands heartily ; wip-
ing them on his — well, he wiped them,

and that is the main thing; besides, his handkerchief had been reduced to a pulp in Gay's service. He combed his hair, pulled up his stockings and tied his shoes neatly, buttoned his jacket closely over his shirt, and was just pinning up the rent in his hat, when Rags considerately brought another suggestion in the shape of an old chicken-wing, with which he brushed every speck of dust from his clothes. This done, and being no respecter of persons, he took the family comb to Rags, who woke the echoes during the operation, and hoped to the Lord that the squirrels would run slowly and that the field-mice would be very tender, to pay him for this.

It was now nearly eight o'clock, and the party descended the hillside and entered the side door of the station.

The day's work had long since begun, and there was the usual din and uproar of rail-road traffic. Trucks, laden high with boxes and barrels, were being driven to the wide doors. The porters were thundering and thumping and lurching the freight from one set of cars into another; their primary objects being to make a racket and demolish raw material, thereby increasing manufacture and export, but incidentally to load or unload as much freight as possible in a given time.

Timothy entered, trundling his carriage, where Lady Gay sat enthroned like a Murray Hill belle on a dog-cart, conscious pride of Sunday hat on week-day morning exuding from every feature; and Rags followed close behind, clean, but with a crushed spirit, which he could stimulate only by the most seductive imaginations. No one molested them, for Timothy was very careful not to get in any one's way. Finally, he drew up in front of a high blackboard, on which the names of various way-stations were printed in gold letters.

CHESTERTOWN
SANDFORD
REEDVILLE
BINGHAM
SKALLOSTOWN
ESBURY
SCRATCH CORNER
HILLSIDE
MOUNTAIN VIEW
EDGEWOOD
PLEASANT RIVER

"The names get nicer and nicer as you read down the line, and the furtherest one of all is the very prettiest, so I guess we 'll go there," thought Timothy, not realizing that his choice was based on most insecure foundations ; and that, for aught he knew, the milk of human kindness might have more cream on it at Scratch Corner than at Pleasant

"I guess we 'll go there"

River, though the latter name was certainly more attractive.

Gay approved of Pleasant River, and so

did Rags; and Timothy moved off down the
station to a place on the open platform
where a train of cars stood ready for starting, the engine at the head gasping and puff-
ing and breathing as hard as if it had an
acute attack of asthma.

"How much does it cost to go to Pleasant
River, please?" asked Tim, bravely, of a
kind-looking man in a blue coat and brass
buttons, who stood by the cars.

"This is a freight train, sonny," replied
the man; "takes four hours to get there.
Better wait till ten forty-five; buy your
ticket up in the station."

"Ten forty-five!" Tim saw visions of
Mrs. Simmons speeding down upon him in
hot pursuit, kindled by Gay's disappearance
into a tardy appreciation of her charms.

The tears stood in his eyes as Gay clam-
bered out of the basket and danced with
impatience, exclaiming, "Gay wants to yide
now! yide now! yide now!"

"Did you want to go sooner?" asked the
man, who seemed to be entirely too much
interested in humanity to succeed in the rail-
road business. "Well, as you seem to have

consid'rable of a family on your hands, I
guess we 'll take you along. Jim, unlock
that car and let these children in, and then
lock it up again. It 's a car we 're taking up
to the end of the road for repairs, bubby,
so the comp'ny 'll give you and your folks a
free ride ! "

Timothy thanked the man in his politest
manner, while Gay pressed a piece of moist
cooky in his hand, and offered him one of
her swan's-down kisses, a favor of which she
was usually as chary as if it had possessed a
market value.

"Are you going to take the dog?" asked
the man, as Rags darted up the steps with
sniffs and barks of ecstatic delight. "He
ain't so handsome but you can get another
easy enough!" (Rags held his breath in
suspense, and wondered if he had been put
under a roaring cataract, and then ploughed
in deep furrows with a sharp-toothed instru-
ment of torture, only to be left behind at
last !)

"That 's just why I take him," said Timothy ; "because he is n't handsome and has
nobody else to love him."

("Not a very polite reason," thought
Rags ; "but anything to go !")

"Well, jump in, dog and all, and they'll
give you the best free ride to the country
you ever had in your life ! Tell 'em it 's all
right, Jim ;" and the train steamed out of
the depot, while the kind man waved his
bandana handkerchief until the children
were out of sight.

SCENE IV

PLEASANT RIVER

Jabe Slocum assumes the Rôle of Guardian Angel

ABE SLOCUM had
been down to Edge-
wood, and was just re-
turning to the White Farm
by way of the cross-roads and
Hard Scrabble schoolhouse. He was in no
hurry, although he always had more work
on hand than he could leave undone for a
month ; and Maria also was taking her own
time, as usual, even stopping now and then
to crop an unusually sweet tuft of grass that
grew within smelling distance, and which no
mare with a driver like Jabe could afford to
pass without notice.

Jabe was ostensibly out on an "errant"
for Miss Avilda Cummins; but, as he had
been in her service for six years, she had no

expectations of his accomplishing anything
beyond getting to a place and getting back
in the same day, the distance covered being
no factor at all in the matter.

One need not apply, however, to Miss
Avilda Cummins for a description of Jabe
Slocum's peculiarities.   They were all so
written upon his face and figure and speech
that the wayfaring man, though a fool, could
not err in his judgment.   He was a long,
loose, knock-kneed, slack-twisted person, and
would have been " longer yit if he hed n't
hed so much turned up for feet " — so Aunt
Hitty Tarbox said.   (Aunt Hitty went from
house to house in Edgewood and Pleasant
River, making over boys' clothes ; and as her
tongue flew as fast as her needle, her sharp
speeches were always in circulation in both
villages.)

Mr. Slocum had sandy hair, high cheek-
bones, a pair of kindly light blue eyes, and
a most unique nose ; I hardly know to what
order of architecture this belonged, — perhaps Old Colonial would describe it as well
as anything else.   It was a wide, flat, well-
ventilated, hospitable edifice, so peculiarly

constructed and applied that Samantha Ann
Ripley (of whom more anon) declared that
"the reason Jabe Slocum ketched cold so
easy was that, if he did n't hold his head jess
so, it kep' a-rainin' in on him!"

His mouth was simply an enormous slit
in his face, and served all the purposes for
which a mouth is presumably intended, save,
perhaps, the trivial one of decoration. In
short (a ludicrously inappropriate word for
the subject), it was a capital medium for
exits and entrances, but no ornament to his
countenance. When Rhapsena Crabb, now
deceased, was first engaged to Jabez Slocum,
Aunt Hitty Tarbox said it beat her "how
Rhapseny ever got over Jabe's mouth;
though she could 'a' got intew it easy 'nough,
or raound it, if she took plenty o' time."
But perhaps Rhapsena appreciated a mouth
(in a husband) that never was given to
"jawin'," and which uttered only kind words
during her brief span of married life. Moreover, there was precious little leisure for
kissing at Pleasant River.

As Jabe had passed the store, a few minutes before, one of the boys had called out,

facetiously, "Say! Shet yer mouth when ye go by the deepot, Laigs ; the train's comin' in !" But he only smiled placidly, though it was an ancient joke, the flavor of which had just fully penetrated the rustic skull ; and the villagers could not resist titillating the sense of humor with it once or twice a month. Neither did Jabez mind being called "Laigs," the local pronunciation of the word "legs ;" in fact, his good humor was too deep to be ruffled. His "cistern of wrathfulness was so small, and the supply pipe so un- ready," that it was next to impossible to put him out, so the natives said.

He was a man of tolerable education ; the only son of his parents, who had endeavored to make great things of him, and might per- haps have succeeded, if he had n't always had so little time at his disposal, — "had n't been so drove," as he expressed it. He went to the village school as regularly as he could not help, that is, as many days as he could not contrive to stay away, until he was fourteen. From there he was sent to the Academy, three miles distant ; but his mo- ther soon found that he could n't make the two trips a day and be "under cover by candlelight;" so the plan of a classical education was abandoned, and he was allowed to speed the home plough, — a profession which he pursued with such moderation that his father, when starting him down a furrow in the morning, used to hang his dinner-pail on his arm, and, bidding him good-by, beg him, with tears in his eyes, to be back before sundown.

At the present moment Jabe was enjoying a cud of Old Virginia plug tobacco, and taking in no more of the landscape than he could avoid, when Maria, having wound up to the top of Marm Berry's hill, in spite of herself walked directly out on one side of the road, and stopped short to make room for the passage of an imposing procession, made up of one clothes-basket on wheels, one baby, one strange boy, and one strange dog.

Jabe, who loved children, eyed the party with some placid interest, but with no undue excitement. Shifting his huge quid, he inquired in his usual leisurely manner, "Which way yer goin', bub, — t' the Swamp or t' the Falls?"

Timothy thought neither sounded especially inviting, but, rapidly choosing the lesser evil, replied, "To the Falls, sir."

"Thy way happens to be my way, 's Rewth said to Naomi; so 'f gittin' over the road 's your objeck, 'n' y' ain't pertickler 'baout the gait ye travel, ye can git in 'n' ride a piece. We don't b'lieve in hurryin,' Mariar 'n' me. Slow 'n' easy goes

"Which way yer goin', bub?"

fur in a day 's our motto.   Can ye git your folks aboard withaout spillin' any of 'em?"

No wonder he asked, for Gay was in such a wild state of excitement that she could hardly be held.

"I can lift Gay up, if you'll please take her, sir," said Timothy; "and if you're quite sure the horse will stand still."

"Bless your soul, she'll stan' all right;

she 'll stan' while you 're gittin' in 'n' consid'rable of a spell afterwards ; in point o'
fact, she likes stan'in' a heap better 'n she
doos goin'. Runnin' away ain't no tempta-
tion to Maria Cummins ; let well enough
alone 's her motto. Jump in, sissy ! There
ye be ! Now git yer baby-shay in the back
of the wagon, bubby, 'n' we 'll be 's snug 's
a bug in a rug."

Timothy, whose creed was simple and
whose beliefs were crystal clear, now felt
that his morning prayer had been heard,
and that the Lord was on his side ; therefore he abandoned all idea of commanding
the situation, and gave himself up to the full
ecstasy of the ride, as they jogged peacefully
along the river road.

Gay held a piece of a rein that peeped
from Jabe's colossal hand (which was said
by the villagers to cover almost as much
territory as the hand of Providence), and
was convinced that she was driving Maria,
an idea that made her speechless with joy.

Rags' wildest dreams of squirrels came
true ; and, reconciled at length to cleanli-
ness, he was capering in and out of the

woods, thinking what an Arabian Nights'
entertainment he would give the Minerva
Court dogs when he returned, if return he
ever must to that miserable, squirrelless
hole.

The meadows on the other side of the
river were gorgeous with yellow buttercups,
and here and there a patch of blue iris or
wild sage. The black cherry trees were
masses of snowy bloom ; the water at the
river's edge held spikes of blue arrowweed
in its crystal shallows ; while the roadside
itself was gay with daisies and feathery
grasses.

In the midst of this loveliness flowed
Pleasant River,

"Vexed in all its seaward course by bridges, dams, and
   mills,"

but finding time, during the busy summer
months, to flush its fertile banks with beauty.

Suddenly (a word that could seldom be
truthfully applied to the description of Jabe
Slocum's movements) the reins were ruth-
lessly drawn from Lady Gay's hands and
wound about the whipstock.

"Gorry !" ejaculated Mr. Slocum, "ef I

hain't left the widder Foss settin' on Aunt
Hitty's hoss-block, 'n' I promised to pick her
up when I come along back! That all comes
o' my drivin' by the store so fast on account
o' the boys hectorin' of me, so 't when I got
to the turn I was so kind of het up I jogged
right along the straight road. Haste makes
waste 's an awful good motto. Pile out,
young ones! It's only half a mile from here
to the Falls, 'n' you'll have to get there on
Shank's mare, for certain!"

So saying, he dumped the astonished children into the middle of the road, from
whence he had plucked them, turned the
docile mare, and with a "Git, Mariar!"
went four miles back to relieve Aunt Hitty's
horse-block from the weight of the widder
Foss (which was no joke!).

This turn of affairs was most unexpected,
and Gay seemed on the point of tears; but
Timothy gathered her a handful of wild-
flowers, wiped the dust from her face, put
on the clean blue gingham apron, and established her in the basket, where she soon fell
asleep, wearied by the excitements of the
day.

Timothy's heart began to be a little troubled as he walked on and on through the leafy woods, trundling the basket behind him. Nothing had gone wrong; indeed, everything had been much easier than he could have hoped. Perhaps it was the weariness that had crept into his legs, and the hollowness that began to appear in his stomach; but, somehow, although in the morning he had expected to find Gay's new adopted mothers beckoning from every window, so that he could scarcely choose between them, he now felt as if the whole race of mothers had suddenly become extinct.

Soon the village came in sight, nestled in the laps of the green hills on both sides of the river. Timothy trudged bravely on, scanning all the dwellings, but finding none of them just the thing. At last he turned deliberately off the main road, where the houses seemed too near together and too near the street for his taste, and trundled his family down a shady sort of avenue, over which the arching elms met and clasped hands.

Rags had by this time lowered his tail

to half-mast, and kept strictly to the beaten
path, notwithstanding manifold temptations
to forsake it. He passed two cats without
a single insulting remark, and his entire de-
meanor was eloquent of nostalgia.

"Oh, dear!" sighed Timothy disconso-
lately; "there's something wrong with all
the places. Either there's no pigeon-house,
like in all the pictures of the country, or
no flower garden, or no chickens, or no lady
at the window, or else there's lots of baby-
clothes hanging on the wash-lines. I don't
believe I shall ever find" —

At this moment a large, comfortable white
house, that had been heretofore hidden by
great trees, came into view. Timothy drew
nearer to the spotless picket fence, and gazed
upon the beauties of the side yard and the
front garden, — gazed and gazed, and fell
desperately in love at first sight.

The whole thing had been made as if to
order; that is all there is to say about it.
There was an orchard, and, oh ecstasy!
what hosts of green apples! There was an
alluring grindstone under one tree, and a
bright blue chair and stool under another;

a thicket of currant and gooseberry bushes,
and a flock of young turkeys ambling awk-
wardly through the barn.   Timothy stepped
gently along in the thick grass, past a pump
and a mossy trough, till a side porch came
into view, with a woman sitting there sewing
bright-colored rags.   A row of shining tin
pans caught the sun's rays, and threw them
back in a thousand glittering prisms of light;
the grasshoppers and crickets chirped sleepily in the warm grass, and a score of tiny
yellow butterflies hovered over a group of
odorous hollyhocks.

Suddenly the person on the porch broke
into a cheerful song, pitched in so high a key
and given with such emphasis that the crickets and grasshoppers retired by mutual con-
sent from any further competition, and the
butterflies suspended operations for several
seconds : —

> " I 'll chase the antelope over the plain,
>   The tiger's cub I 'll bind with a chain,
>   And the wild gazelle with the silv'ry feet,
>   I 'll bring to thee for a playmate sweet."

Timothy listened intently for some moments, not understanding the words, unless

the lady happened to be in the menagerie
business, which he thought unlikely, but de-
lightful should it prove true.

His eye then fell on a little marble slab
under a tree in a shady corner of the orchard.

"That must be a country doorplate," he
thought; "yes, it's got the lady's name,

" That must be a country doorplate "

'Martha Cummins,' printed on it.   Now I'll
know what to call her."

He crept softly on to the front side of the
house.   There were flower beds, a lovable
white cat snoozing on the doorsteps, and a
lady sitting at the open window knitting, —
in all probability Gay's adopted mother.

At this vision Timothy's heart beat so hard
against his jacket that he could only stagger
back to the basket, where Rags and Lady
Gay were snuggled together fast asleep.   He
anxiously scanned Gay's face ; moistened his
rag of a handkerchief at the only available
source of supply; scrubbed an atrocious dirt
spot from the tip of her spirited nose ; and
then, dragging the basket along the path
leading to the front gate, he opened it and
went in, mounted the steps, plied the brass
knocker, and waited in childlike faith for a
summons to enter in and make himself at
home.

SCENE V

THE WHITE FARM. AFTERNOON

*Timothy finds a House in which He thinks a Baby is
needed, but the Inmates do not entirely agree
with Him*

EANWHILE, Miss Avil-
da Cummins had left her
window and gone into
the next room for a skein
of yarn. She answered the knock,
however ; and, opening the door,
stood rooted to the threshold in
speechless astonishment, very much as if
she had seen the shades of her ancestors
drawn up in line in the dooryard.

Off went Timothy's hat. He had not seen
the lady's face very clearly when she was
knitting at the window, or he would never
have dared to knock ; but it was too late to
retreat. Looking straight into her cold eyes
with his own shining gray ones, he said
bravely, but with a trembling voice, " Please
— do you need any babies here, if you
please ? " (Need any babies ! What an inappropriate, nonsensical expression, to be
sure ; as if a baby in a house were something

exquisitely indispensable, like the breath of life, for instance!)

No answer. Miss Vilda was trying to assume command of her scattered faculties and find some clue to the situation. Timothy concluded that she was not, after all, the lady of the house; and, remembering the marble doorplate in the orchard, tried again. "Does Miss Martha Cummins live here, if you please?" (Oh, Timothy! what induced you, in this crucial moment of your life, to touch upon that sorest spot in Miss Vilda's memory?)

"What do you want?" she faltered.

"I want to get somebody to adopt my baby," he said; "if you have n't got any of your own, you could n't find one half as dear and as pretty as she is, and she does n't freckle so much in the winter time. You need n't have me, too, you know, unless you need me to help take care of her."

"You 're very kind," Miss Avilda answered sarcastically, preparing to shut the door upon the strange child; "but I don't think I care to adopt any babies this afternoon, thank you. You 'd better run right back home to your mother, if you 've got one, and know where 't is, anyhow."

"But I — have n't!" cried poor Timothy, with a sudden and unpremeditated burst of tears at the failure of his hopes, for he was half child as well as half hero. At this juncture Gay opened her eyes and burst into a wild howl at the unwonted sight of Timothy's grief; while Rags, who was full of exquisite sensibility, and quite ready to weep with those who did weep, lifted up his woolly head and added his piteous wails to the concert. It was a *tableau vivant.*

"Samanthy Ann!" called Miss Vilda excitedly; "Samanthy Ann! Come right in here and tell me what to do!"

The person thus adjured flew in from the porch, leaving a serpentine trail of red, yellow, and blue rags in her wake. "Land o' liberty!" she exclaimed, as she surveyed the group. "Where 'd they come from, and what air they tryin' to act out?"

"This boy 's a baby agent, as near as I can make out; he wants I should adopt this red-headed baby, but says I ain't obliged to take him too, and makes out they have n't

got any home. I told him I wan't adoptin'
any babies just now, and at that he burst
out cryin', and the other two followed suit.
Now, have the three of 'em just escaped
from some asylum, or are they too little to
be lunatics?"

Timothy dried his tears in order that Gay
should be comforted and appear at her best,
and said penitently: "I cried before I
thought, because Gay has n't had anything
but cookies to eat since last night, and
she 'll have no place to sleep unless you 'll
let us stay here just till morning. We
went by all the other houses, and chose this
one because everything was just what we
wanted."

"Nothin' but cookies sence — Land o' liberty!" ejaculated Samantha Ann, starting
for the kitchen.

"Come back here, Samanthy! Don't you
leave me alone with 'em, and don't let 's have
all the neighbors runnin' in. Take 'em into
the kitchen and give 'em somethin' to eat,
and we 'll see about the rest afterwards."

Gay kindled at the first casual mention of
food, and trying to clamber out of the basket,

fell over the edge, thumping her head smartly
on the stone steps. Miss Vilda covered her
face with her hands, and waited shudder-
ingly for another yell, as the child's carna-
tion stockings and terra-cotta head mingled
wildly in the air. But Lady Gay disen-
tangled herself, and laughed the merriest
burst of laughter that ever woke the echoes.
That was a joke ; her life was full of them,
served fresh every day, for no sort of ad-
versity could long have power over such
a nature as hers. "Come get supper," she
cooed, putting her hand
in Samantha's; adding
that the "nasty lady
need n't come," a re-
mark that happily es-
caped detection, as it
was rendered in very un-
intelligible "early Eng-
lish."

In the Kitchen

Miss Avilda tottered
into the darkened sit-
ting-room and sank on
to a black hair-cloth sofa, while Samantha
ushered the wanderers into the sunny kitchen,

muttering to herself: "Wall, I vow! travelin' over the country all alone, 'n' not knee-high to a toad! They're sendin' out awful young tramps this season, but they shan't go away from this house hungry, not if I know it."

Accordingly she set out a plentiful supply of bread and butter, gingerbread, pie, and milk, put a tin plate of cold hash in the shed for Rags, sweeping him out to it with a corn broom, violently, as is the manner in that section, and, telling the children comfortably to cram their "everlastin' little bread-baskets full," returned to the sitting-room.

"Now, whatever makes you so panicky, Vildy? Did n't you never see a tramp before, for pity's sake? And if you 're scar't for fear I can't handle 'em alone, why, Jabe 'll be comin' along soon. The prospeck of gittin' to bed 's the only thing that 'll make him 'n' Maria hurry; 'n' they 'll both be cal'latin' on that by this time!"

"Samanthy Ann, the first question that that boy asked me was, if Miss Martha Cummins lived here. Now, what do you make of that?"

Samantha looked as astonished as anybody could wish. "Asked if Marthy Cummins lived here? How under the canopy did he ever hear Marthy's name? Wall, somebody told him to ask, that 's all there is about it, and what harm was there in it, anyhow?"

"Oh, I don't know, I don't know; but the minute that boy looked up at me and asked for Martha Cummins, the old trouble, that I thought was dead and buried years ago, started right up in my heart and begun to ache just as if it all happened yesterday."

"Now keep stiddy, Vildy, what could happen?" urged Samantha.

"Why, it flashed across my mind in a minute," and here Miss Vilda lowered her voice to a whisper, "that perhaps Martha's baby did n't die as they told her."

"But, land o' liberty, s'posin' it did n't! Poor Marthy died herself more 'n twenty years ago."

"I know; but supposing her baby grew up before it died, and left one of these children to roam round the world afoot and alone."

"You 're cal'latin' dreadful close, 'pears to

me; now, don't go sposin' any more things.
You 're makin' out one o' them yellow-cov-
ered books, sech as the summer boarders
bring out here to read; always chock full of
doin's that never would come to pass in this
or any other Christian country.   You jest
lay down and snuff your camphire, an' I 'll
go out an' pump that boy drier 'n a sand
heap!''

Now Miss Avilda Cummins was unmarried
by every implication of her being, as Henry
James would say: but Samantha Ann Ripley was a spinster purely by accident.   She
had seldom been exposed to the witcheries
of children, or she would have known long
before this that, so far as she was personally
concerned, they would always prove irresistible.   She marched into the kitchen like a
general resolved upon the extinction of the
enemy.   She walked out again, half an hour
later, with the very teeth of her resolve
drawn, but so painlessly that she had not
been aware of the operation!   She marched
in a woman of single purpose; she came out
a double-faced diplomatist, with the seeds of

sedition and conspiracy lurking, all unsus-
pected, in her heart.

The cause? Nothing more than a dozen
trifles light as air.
Timothy had sat
upon a little wood-
en stool at her feet;
had rested his arms
on her knees and
looked up into her
kind, rosy face with
a pair of liquid
eyes like gray-blue
lakes, eyes which
seemed and were
the very windows

Timothy telling his Story

of his soul. He had sat there telling his
wee bit of a story; just a vague, shadowy,
plaintive, uncomplaining scrap of a story,
without beginning, plot, or ending, but every
word in it set Samantha Ann Ripley's heart
throbbing.

Gay, who knew a good thing when she saw
it, had climbed up into her capacious lap,
and, not being denied, had cuddled her head
into that "gracious hollow" in Samantha's

shoulder that had somehow missed the pressure of the childish heads that should have lain there. Then Samantha's arm had finally crept round the wheedlesome bit of soft humanity, and before she knew it the old flag-bottomed chair was swaying gently to and fro, to and fro, to and fro; and the wooden rockers creaked more sweetly than ever they had creaked before, for they were singing their first cradle song!

Then Gay heaved a great sigh of unspeakable satisfaction, and closed her lovely eyes. She had been born with a desire to be cuddled, and had had precious little experience of it. At the sound of this happy sigh and the sight of the child's flower face, with the upward curling lashes on the pink cheeks, the oval snow-drift of the chin, the moist tendrils of hair on the white forehead, and the helpless, unaccustomed, clinging touch of the baby arm about her neck, I cannot tell you the why or wherefore, but old memories and new desires began to stir in Samantha Ann Ripley's heart. In short, she had met the enemy, and she was theirs!

Presently Gay was laid upon the old-fash-

ioned settle, and Samantha stationed herself
where she could keep the flies off her by
waving a palm-leaf fan.

"Now, there's one thing more I want you
to tell me," said she, after she had possessed
herself of Timothy's unhappy past, uncertain
present, and still more dubious future; "and
that is, what made you ask for Miss Marthy
Cummins when you come to the door?"

"Why, I thought it was the lady-of-the-
house's name," said Timothy; "I saw it on
her doorplate."

"But we ain't got any doorplate, to begin
with."

"Not a silver one on your door, like they
have in the city; but isn't that white
marble piece in the yard a doorplate? It's
got 'Martha Cummins, aged 17,' on it. I
thought may be in the country they had
them in their gardens; only I thought it
was queer they put their ages on them, because they'd have to be scratched out every
little while, wouldn't they?"

"My grief!" ejaculated Samantha: "for
pity's sake, don't you know a tombstun
when you see it?"

"What is a tombstun?"

"Land sakes! what do you know, any-way? Did n't you never see a graveyard where folks is buried?"

"I never went to the graveyard, but I know where it is, and I know about people's being buried. Flossy is going to be buried. So the white stone shows the places where the people are put, and tells their names, does it? Why, it is a kind of a doorplate, after all, don't you see? — Who is Martha Cummins, aged 17?"

"She was Miss Vildy's sister that went to the city, and then come home and died here, long years ago. Miss Vildy set great store by her, and can't bear to have her name spoke; so remember what I say. — Now, this 'Flossy' you tell me about (of all the fool names I ever hearn tell of, that beats all, — sounds like a wax doll, with her clo'es sewed on!), was she a young woman?"

"I don't know whether she was young or not," said Tim, in a puzzled tone. "She had young yellow hair, and very young shiny teeth, white as china; but her neck was crackled underneath, like Miss Vilda's. It had no kissing places in it like Gay's."

"Well, you stay here in the kitchen a spell now, 'n' don't let in that rag-dog o' yourn till he stops scratchin', if he keeps it up till the crack o' doom ;—he 's got to be learned better manners. Now, I 'll go in 'n' talk to Miss Vildy. She may keep you over night, 'n' she may not ; I ain't noways sure. You started in wrong foot foremost."

SCENE VI

THE WHITE FARM. EVENING

*Timothy, Lady Gay, and Rags prove faithful to each
other*

SAMANTHA went into the sitting-room and told the whole story to Miss Avilda; told it simply and plainly, for she was not given to arabesques in language, and then waited for a response.

"Well, what do you advise doin'?" asked Miss Cummins nervously.

"I don't feel comp'tent to advise, Vilda; the house ain't mine, nor yet the beds that's in it, nor the victuals in the butt'ry; but as a professin' Christian and member of the Orthodox Church in good and reg'lar standin', you can't turn them children ou'doors when it's comin' on dark and they ain't got no place to sleep."

"Plenty of good Orthodox folks turned their backs on Martha when she was in trouble."

"There may be Orthodox hogs, for all I know," replied the blunt Samantha, who frequently called spades shovels in her search after absolute truth of statement, "but that ain't no reason why we should copy after 'em 's I know of."

"I don't propose to take in two strange children and saddle myself with 'em for days, or weeks, perhaps," said Miss Cummins coldly, "but I tell you what I will do. Supposing we send the boy over to Squire Bean's. It's near hayin' time, and he may take him in to help round and do chores. Then we'll tell him before he goes that we'll keep the baby as long as he gets a chance to work anywheres near. That will give us time to look round for some place for 'em and find out whether they've told us the truth."

"And if Squire Bean won't take the boy?" asked Samantha, with as much indifference as she could assume.

"Well, I suppose there's nothing for it but he must come back here and sleep. I'll go out and tell him so, — I declare I feel as weak as if I'd had a spell of sickness!"

Timothy bore the news better than Samantha had feared. Squire Bean's farm did not look so very far away ; his heart was at rest about Gay ; he felt that he could find a shelter for himself somewhere, and anything was better than a Home with a capital H.

"Now, how 'll the baby act when she wakes up and finds you 're gone?" inquired Miss Vilda anxiously, as Timothy took his hat and bent down to kiss the sleeping child.

"Well, I don't know exactly," answered Timothy, "because she 's always had me, you see. But I think she 'll be all right, now that she knows you a little, if I can see her every day. She never cries except once in a long while when she gets mad ; and if you 're careful how you behave, she 'll hardly ever get mad at you."

"Well I vow!" exclaimed Miss Vilda with a grim glance at Samantha, "I guess she 'll have to do the behavin'."

So Timothy was shown the way across the fields to Squire Bean's. Samantha accompanied him to the back gate, where she gave him three doughnuts and a sneaking kiss, watching him out of sight under the pretense of taking the towels and napkins off the grass.

It was nearly nine o'clock and quite dark when Timothy stole again to the little gate of the White Farm. The feet that had traveled so courageously over the mile walk to Squire Bean's had come back again slowly and wearily; for it is one thing to be shod

with the sandals of hope, and quite another to tread upon the leaden soles of disappointment.

He leaned upon the white picket gate listening to the chirp of the frogs and looking at the fireflies as they hung their gleaming

Timothy goes to Squire Bean's

lamps here and there in the tall grass. Then he crept round to the side door, to implore the kind offices of the mediator before he entered the presence of the judge, whom he assumed to be sitting in awful state somewhere in the front part of the house. He lifted the latch noiselessly and entered. Oh horror! Miss Avilda herself was sprinkling clothes at the great table on one side of the room.

There was a moment of silence.

"He would n't have me," said Timothy simply, "he said I was n't big enough to be any good. I offered him Gay, too, but he did n't want her either, and if you please, I would rather sleep on the sofa so as not to be any more trouble."

"You won't do any such thing," responded Miss Vilda briskly. "You 've got a royal welcome this time, sure, and I guess you can earn your lodging fast enough. You hear that?" and she opened the door that led into the upper part of the house.

A piercing shriek floated down into the kitchen, and another on the heels of that, and then another. Every drop of blood in Timothy's spare body rushed to his pale face. "Is she being whipped?" he whispered, with set lips.

"No; she needs it bad enough, but we ain't savages. She 's only got the pretty temper that matches her hair, just as you

said. I guess we have n't been behavin' to
suit her."

"Can I go up ? She 'll stop in a minute
when she sees me. She never went to bed
without me before, and truly, truly, she is n't
a cross baby ! "

"Come right along and welcome ; just so
long as she has to stay you 're invited to
visit with her. Land sakes ! the neighbors
will think we 're killin' pigs !" and Miss
Vilda started upstairs to show Timothy the
way.

Gay was sitting up in bed and the faithful
Samantha Ann was seated beside her with
a lapful of bribes, — apples, seed-cakes, an
illustrated Bible, a thermometer, an ear of
red corn, and a large stuffed green bird, the
glory of the "keeping room" mantelpiece.

The bribes were all useless. A whole
aviary of highly colored songsters would not
have assuaged Gay's woe at that moment.
Every effort at conciliation was met with
the one plaint : "I want my Timfy ! I want
my Timfy ! "

At the first sight of the beloved form, Gay
flung the sacred bird into the furthest corner

of the room, and burst into a wild sob of delight as she threw herself into Timothy's loving arms.

Fifteen minutes later peace had descended on the troubled homestead, and Samantha went into the sitting-room and threw herself into the depths of the high-backed rocker. "Land o' liberty! perhaps I ain't het up!" she ejaculated, as she wiped her brow and fanned herself vigorously with her apron. "I tell you what, at five o'clock I was dreadful sorry I had n't took Dave Milliken, but now I 'm plaguey glad I did n't! Still" (and here she tried to smooth the green bird's ruffled plumage and restore him to his perch under the revered glass case), "still, children will be children."

"Some of 'em 's considerable more like wild cats," said Miss Avilda briefly.

"You just go upstairs now, and see if you find anything that looks like wild cats; but 't any rate, wild cats or tame cats, we would n't dass turn 'em ou'doors this time o' night for fear of flyin' in the face of Providence. If it 's a stint He 's set us, I don't see but we 've got to work it out somehow,"

"I 'd rather have some other stint."

"To be sure!" retorted Samantha vigorously. "I never see anybody yet that did n't want to pick out her own stint; but mebbe if we got just the one we wanted it would n't be no stint! — Land o' liberty, what 's that!"

There was a crash of falling tin pans, and Samantha flew to investigate the cause. About ten minutes later she returned, more heated than ever, and threw herself for the second time into the high-backed rocker.

"That dog 's been givin' me a chase, I can tell you! He clawed and scratched so in the shed that I put him in the wood-house; then he went and clim' up on that carpenter's bench, and pitched out that little winder at the top, and fell on to the milk-pan shelf and scattered every last one of 'em, and then upsot all my cans of termatter plants. But I could n't find him, high nor low. All at once I see by the dirt on the floor that he 'd squirmed himself through the skeeter-nettin' door int' the house, and then I surmised where he was. Sure enough, I crep' upstairs and there he was, layin' between the two children as snug as you please. He was

snorin' like a pirate when I found him, but
when I stood over the bed with a candle I
could see 't his wicked little eyes was wide
open, and he was jest makin' b'lieve sleep in
hopes I 'd leave him where he was. Well, I
yanked him out quicker 'n scat, 'n' locked
him in the old chicken house, so I guess
he 'll stay out, now. For folks that claim to
be no blood relation, I declare him 'n' the
boy 'n' the baby beats anything I ever come
across for bein' fond of one 'nother!"

There were dreams at the White Farm
that night. Timothy went to sleep with a
prayer on his lips ; a prayer that God would
excuse him for speaking of Martha's doorplate, and a most imploring postscript to
the effect that God would please make Miss
Vilda into a mother for Gay ; thinking as he
floated off into the land of Nod, "It 'll be
awful hard work, but I don't suppose He
cares how hard 't is!"

Lady Gay dreamed of driving beautiful
white horses beside sparkling waters . . .
and through flowery meadows. . . . And
great green birds perched on all the trees
and flew towards her as if to peck the cher-

ries of her lips . . . but when she tried to beat them off they all turned into Timothys and she hugged them close to her heart. . . .

Rags' visions were gloomy, for he knew not whether the Lady with the Firm Hand would free him from his prison in the morning, or whether he was there for all time. . . . But there were intervals of bliss when his fancies took a brighter turn . . . when Hope smiled . . . and he bit the white cat's

Rags' Dream

tail . . . and chased the infant turkeys . . . and found sweet, juicy, delicious bones in unexpected places . . . and even inhaled, in exquisite anticipation, the fragrance of one particularly succulent bone that he had hidden under Miss Vilda's bed.

Sleep carried Samantha so many years back into the past that she heard the blithe din of carpenters hammering and sawing on a little house that was to be hers, his, *theirs*.

. . . And as she watched them, with all
sorts of maidenly hopes about the home
that was to be . . . some one stole up behind and caught her at it, and she ran away
blushing . . . and some one followed her
. . . and they watched the carpenters together. . . . Somebody else lived in the little house now, and Samantha never blushed
any more, but that part was mercifully hidden in the dream. . . . It is, sometimes.

Miss Vilda's slumber was troubled. She
seemed to be walking through peaceful
meadows, brown with autumn, when all at
once there rose in the path steep hills and
rocky mountains. . . . She felt too tired and
too old to climb, but there was nothing else
to be done. . . . And just as she began the
toilsome ascent, a little child appeared, and
catching her helplessly by the skirts im-
plored to be taken with her. . . . And she
refused and went on alone . . . but, miracle
of miracles, when she reached the crest of
the first hill the child was there before her,
still beseeching to be carried. . . . But again
she refused, and again she wearily climbed
the heights alone, always meeting the child

when she reached their summits, and always
enacting the same scene. . . . At last she
cried in despair, "Ask me no more, for I
have not strength enough even for my own
needs!" . . . And the child said, "I will
help you;" and straightway crept into her
arms and nestled there as one who would not
be denied . . . and she took up her burden
and walked. . . . And as she climbed, the
weight grew lighter and lighter, till at length
the clinging arms seemed to give her peace
and strength . . . and when she neared the
crest of the highest mountain she felt new
life throbbing in her veins and new hopes
stirring in her heart, and she remembered
no more the pain and weariness of her journey. . . . And suddenly an angel appeared
to her and tracing the letters of a word upon
her forehead, took the child from her arms
and disappeared. . . . And the angel had the
lovely smile and sad eyes of her dead sister,
Martha . . . and the word she traced on Miss
Vilda's forehead was "Inasmuch"!

SCENE VII

THE OLD HOMESTEAD

Mistress and Maid find to their Amazement that a Child, more than all other Gifts, brings Hope with it and forward looking Thoughts

I T was called the White Farm, not because white was an unusual color in Pleasant River. Two houses out of every twenty in the village were made of brick and the other eighteen were painted white, for it had not then entered the casual mind that any other course was desirable or possible. Occasionally a man of riotous imagination would substitute two shades of buff, or make the back of his barn red, but the spirit of invention stopped there and the majority of sane people went on painting white. Miss Avilda Cummins, however, was blessed with a larger income than most of the inhabitants of Pleasant River, and all her buildings, the great house, the sheds, the carriage and dairy houses, the fences and the barn, were always kept in a

state of dazzling purity; "as if," the neighbors declared, "S'manthy Ann Ripley went
over 'em every morning with a dust-cloth."

It was merely an accident that the carriage and work horses chanced to be white,
and that the original white cats of the family
kept on having white kittens to decorate the
front doorsteps. It was not accident, however, but design, that caused Jabe Slocum
to scour the country for a good white cow
and persuade Miss Cummins to swap off the
old red one, so that the "critters" in the
barn should match the rest of the establish-
ment.

Miss Avilda had been born at the White
Farm; her father and mother had been taken
from there to the old country churchyard,
and "Martha, aged 17," poor, pretty, willful
Martha, the greatest pride and greatest sorrow of the family, was lying under the apple-
trees in the garden.

Here also the little Samantha Ann Ripley
had come as a child years ago, to be play-
mate, nurse, and companion to Martha, and
here she had stayed ever since, as friend,
adviser, and "company-keeper" to the lonely

Miss Cummins. Nobody in Pleasant River would have dared to think of her as anybody's "hired help," though she did receive bed and board, and a certain sum yearly for her services; for she lived with Miss Cummins on equal terms, as was the custom in the good old New England villages, doing the lion's share of the work, and marking her sense of the situation by washing the dishes while Miss Avilda wiped them, and by never suffering her to feed the pig or go down cellar.

Theirs had been a dull sort of life, in which little had happened to make them grow into sympathy with the outside world. All the sweetness of Miss Avilda's nature had turned to bitterness and gall after Martha's disgrace, sad home-coming, and death. There had been much to forgive, and she had not had the grace nor the strength to forgive it until it was too late. The mystery of death had unsealed her eyes, and there had been a moment when the sad and bitter woman might have been drawn closer to the great Father-heart, there to feel the throb of a Divine compassion that would have sweet-

ened the trial and made the burden lighter.
The minister of the parish proved a sorry
comforter and adviser in these hours of trial.
The Reverend Joshua Beckwith, whose view
of God's universe was about as broad as if he
had lived on the inside of his own pork-bar-
rel, had cherished certain strong and unre-
lenting opinions concerning Martha's final
destination which were not shared by Miss
Cummins. There was a long and heated
argument in the parlor, in the course of
which the Family Bible, the Concordance,
and Barnes's Notes were liberally drawn
upon by the parson. At its close Miss
Avilda announced her intention of having
nothing more to do with church members.
Martha, therefore, was not laid with the
elect, but was put to rest in the orchard,
under the kindly, untheological shade of the
apple-trees, that scattered their tinted blos-
soms over her little white headstone, shed
their fragrance about her quiet grave, and
dropped their ruddy fruit in the high grass
that covered it, just as tenderly and respect-
fully as if they had been regulation willows.
The Reverend Joshua thus succeeded in dry-

ing up the springs
of human sympa-
thy in Miss Avil-
da's heart when
most she needed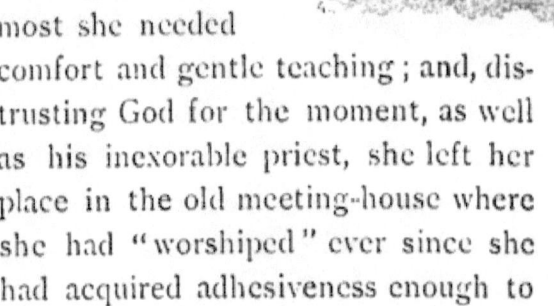
comfort and gentle teaching ; and, dis-
trusting God for the moment, as well
as his inexorable priest, she left her
place in the old meeting-house where
she had "worshiped" ever since she
had acquired adhesiveness enough to
stick to a pew, and was not seen there again
for many years. The Reverend Joshua had
died, as all men must and as most men
should, and a mild voiced successor reigned
in his place, so the Cummins pew was occu-
pied once more.

Samantha Ann Ripley had had her heart
history too, — one of a different kind. She
had "kept company" with David Milliken
for a little matter of twenty years, off and
on, and Miss Avilda had expected at various
times to lose her friend and helpmate ; but
fear of this calamity had at length been quite
put to rest by the fourth and final rupture of
the bond, five years before.

There had always been a family feud between the Ripleys and the Millikens; so
when the young people took it into their
heads to fall in love with each other in spite
of precedent and prejudice, they found that
the course of true love ran in anything but
a true channel. It was, in fact, a sort of village Montague and Capulet affair ; but David
and Samantha were no Romeo and Juliet.
The climate and general conditions of life at
Pleasant River were not favorable to the de-
velopment of such exotics. The old people
interposed barriers between the young ones
as long as they lived ; and when they died,
Dave Milliken's spirit was broken, and he
began to annoy the valiant Samantha by
what she called his "meechin'" ways. In
one of his moments of weakness he took a
widowed sister to live with him, a certain
Mrs. Pettigrove, of Edgewood, who inherited
the Milliken objection to Ripleys, and who
widened the breach and brought Samantha to
the point of final and decisive rupture. The
last straw was the statement, sown broadcast
by Mrs. Pettigrove, "that Samanthy Ann
Ripley's father never would 'a' died if he 'd

ever had any doctorin'; but 't was the gospel truth that they never had nobody to 'tend him but a hom'pathy man from Scratch Corner, who, of course, bein' a hom'path, did n't know no more about doctorin' 'n Cooper's cow."

Samantha told David after this "she did n't want to hear him open his mouth again, nor none of his folks; she was through with the whole lot of 'em forever and ever, 'n' she wished to the Lord she 'd had sense enough to put her foot down fifteen years ago, 'n' she hoped he 'd enjoy bein' trod underfoot for the rest of his natural life, 'n' she would n't speak to him again if she met him in her porridge dish." She then slammed the door and went upstairs to cry as if she were sixteen, as she watched him out of sight. Poor Dave Milliken! just sweet and earnest and strong enough to suffer at being worsted by circumstances, but never quite strong enough to conquer them.

It was to this household that Timothy had brought his child for adoption.

When Miss Avilda opened her eyes the morning after the arrival of the children, she tried to remember whether anything had happened to give her such a strange feeling of altered conditions. It was Saturday, baking day, — that could n't be it, — and she gazed at the little dimity-curtained window and at the picture of the Death-bed of Calvin, and wondered what was the matter.

Just then a child's laugh, bright, merry, tuneful, infectious, rang out from some distant room, and it all came back to her as Samantha Ann opened the door and peered in.

"I 've got breakfast 'bout ready," she said ; "but I wish, soon 's you 're dressed, you 'd step down 'n' see to it, 'n' let me wash the baby. I guess water was skerse where she come from !"

" They 're awake, are they ? "

"Awake ? Land o' liberty ! As soon as 't was light, and before the boy had opened his eyes, Gay was up 'n' poundin' on all the doors, 'n' hollerin' 'S'manfy' (beats all how she got holt o' my name so quick !), so 't I thought sure she 'd disturb your sleep. See here, Vildy, we want those children should look respectable the few days they 're here. I don't see how we can rig out the boy, but there 's those old things of Marthy's in the attic ; seems like it might be a blessin' on 'em if we used 'em this way."

" I thought of it myself in the night," answered Vilda briefly. " You 'll find the key of the trunk in the light-stand drawer. You see to the children, and I 'll get breakfast on the table. Has Jabe come ? "

" No ; he sent a boy to milk, 'n' said he 'd be right along. You know what that means ! "

Miss Vilda moved about the immaculate kitchen, frying potatoes and making tea, setting on extra portions of bread and doughnuts and a huge pitcher of milk ; while various noises, strange enough in that quiet house, floated down from above.

" This is dreadful hard on Samanthy," she reflected. " I don't know 's I 'd ought to have put it on her, knowing how she hates confusion and company, and all that ; but she seemed to think we 'd got to tough it out for a spell, any way ; though I don't expect her temper 'll stand the strain very long."

The fact was, Samantha was banging doors

and slatting tin pails about furiously to keep
up an ostentatious show of ill humor. She
tried her best to grunt with displeasure when
Gay, seated in a wash-tub, crowed and beat
the water with her dimpled hands so that it
splashed all over the carpet ; but all the time
there was such a joy tugging at her heart-
strings as they had not felt for years.

When the bath was over, clean petticoats
and ankle-ties were chosen out of the old
leather trunk, and finally a little blue and
white lawn dress.   It was too long in the
skirt, and pending the moment when Samantha should "take a tack in it," it anticipated
the present fashion, and made Lady Gay
look more like a disguised princess than ever.
The gown was low-necked and short-sleeved,
in the old style, and Samantha was in despair till she found some little embroidered
muslin capes and full undersleeves, with
which she covered Gay's pink neck and arms.
These things of beauty so wrought upon the
child's excitable nature that she could hardly
keep still long enough to have her hair
curled ; and Samantha, as the shining rings
dropped off her horny forefinger, was wrest-

ling with the Evil One in the shape of a little
box of jewelry that she had found with the
clothing. She knew that the wish was a
vicious one and that such gewgaws were out
of place on a little pauper just taken in for
the night; but her fingers trembled with desire to fasten the lit-
tle gold ears of corn
on the shoulders,
or tie the strings of
coral beads around
the child's pretty
throat.

When the toilet
was completed, and
Samantha was emp-
tying the tub, Gay

Gay's Toilet

climbed on the bureau and imprinted sloppy
kisses of sincere admiration on the radiant
reflection of herself in the little looking-
glass; then, getting down again, she seized
her heap of Minerva Court clothes before
the astonished Samantha could interpose,
and flung them out of the second story window, where they fell on the top of the lilac
bushes.

"Me does n't like nasty old dress," she explained, with a dazzling smile that was a justification in itself; "me likes pretty new dress!" and then, with one hand reaching up to the door-knob and the other throwing disarming kisses to Samantha, — "By-by! Lady Gay go circus now! S'manfy come take Lady Gay to circus!"

There was no time for discipline then, and she was borne to the breakfast-table, where Timothy was already making acquaintance with Miss Vilda.

Samantha entered, and Vilda, glancing at her nervously, perceived with relief that she was "taking things easy." Ah! but it was lucky for poor David Milliken that he could not see her at that moment. Her whole face had relaxed; her mouth was no longer a thin, hard line, but had a certain curve and fullness, borrowed perhaps from the warmth of innocent baby kisses. Embarrassment and stifled joy had brought a rosier color to her cheek; Gay's vandal hand had ruffled the smoothness of her sandy locks, so that a few stray hairs were absolutely curling with amazement that they had escaped from their sleek bondage; in a word, Samantha Ann Ripley was lovely and lovable!

Timothy had no eyes for any one save his beloved Gay, at whom he gazed with unspeakable admiration, thinking it impossible that any human being with a single eye in his head could refuse to take such an angel when it was in the market.

Gay, not being used to a regular morning toilet, had fought against it valiantly at first; but the tonic of the bath itself and the exercise of war had brought the color to her cheeks and the brightness to her eyes. She had forgiven Samantha, she was ready to be on good terms with Miss Vilda, she was at peace with all the world. That she was eating the bread of dependence did not trouble her in the least! No royal visitor, conveying honor by her mere presence, could have carried off a delicate situation with more distinguished grace and ease. She was perched on a Webster's Unabridged Dictionary, and immediately began blowing bubbles in her mug of milk in the most reprehensible fashion; glancing up after each naughty effort with an irrepressible gurgle of laughter, in

which she looked so bewitching, even with a
milky crescent over her red mouth, that she
would have melted the heart of the most
predestinate old misogynist in Christendom.

Timothy was not so entirely at his ease.
His eyes had looked into life only a few
more summers, but their "radiant morning
visions" had been dispelled; experience had
tempered joy.   Gay, however, had not ar-
rived at an age where people's motives can
be suspected for an instant.   If there had
been any possible plummet with which to
sound the depths of her unconscious philoso-
phy, she apparently looked upon herself as a
guest out of heaven, flung down upon this
hospitable planet with the single responsi-
bility of enjoying its treasures.

O happy heart of childhood! Your simple creed is rich in faith, and trust, and hope.
You have not learned that the children of a
common Father can do aught but love and
help each other.

SCENE VIII

THE OLD GARDEN

Jabe and Samantha exchange Hostilities, and the Former says a Good Word for the Little Wanderers

"GOD Almighty first planted a garden, and it is indeed the purest of all human pleasures," said Lord Bacon ; and Miss Vilda would have agreed with him. Her garden was not simply the purest of all her pleasures, it was her only one ; the love that other people gave to family, friends, or kindred she lavished on her posies.

It was a dear, old-fashioned, odorous garden, where Dame Nature had never been forced, but only assisted, to do her duty. Miss Vilda sowed her seeds in the spring-time wherever there chanced to be room, and they came up and flourished and went to seed just as they liked, these being the only duties required of them. Two splen-

did groups of fringed "pinics," the pride of
Miss Avilda's heart, grew just inside the
gate, and hard by the handsomest dahlias in
the village, quilled beauties like carved ro-
settes of gold and coral and ivory. There
was plenty of feathery "sparrowgrass," so
handy to fill the black and yawning chasms
of summer fireplaces and furnish green for
"boquets." There was a stray peach or
greengage tree here and there, and if a plain,
well-meaning carrot chanced to lift its leaves
among the poppies, why, they were all the
children of the same mother, and Miss Vilda
was not the woman to root out the invader
and fling it into the ditch. There was a bed
of yellow tomatoes, where, in the season, a
hundred tiny golden balls hung among the
green leaves ; and just beside them, in
friendly equality, a tangle of pink sweet-
williams, fragrant phlox, delicate bride's-tears,
canterbury bells blue as the June sky, none-
so-pretties, gay cockscombs, and flaunting
marigolds, which would insist on coming up
all together, summer after summer, regard-
less of color harmonies. Last, but not least,
there was a patch of sweet peas,

"on tiptoe for a flight,
With wings of gentle flush o'er delicate white."

These dispensed their sweet odors so gener-
ously that it was a favorite diversion among
the village children to stand in rows outside
the fence, and, elevating their bucolic noses,
simultaneously "sniff Miss Cummins' peas."
The garden was large enough to have little
hills and dales of its own, and its banks
sloped gently down to the river. There was
a gnarled apple-tree hidden by a luxuriant
wild grapevine, a fit bower for a "lov'd Celia"
or a "fair Rosamond." There was a spring,
whose crystal waters were "cabined, cribbed,
confined," within a barrel sunk in the earth;
a brook singing its way among the alder
bushes and dripping here and there into
pools, over which the blue harebells leaned
to see themselves. There was also a summer-house on the brink of the hill; a weather-
stained affair, with a hundred names carved
on its venerable lattices, — names of youths
and maidens who had stood there in the
moonlight and plighted rustic vows.

If you care to feel a warm glow in the re-
gion of your heart, imagine little Timothy

Jessup sent to play in that garden, — sent
to play for almost the first time in his life!
Imagine it, I ask, for there are some things
too sweet to prick with a pen-point.   The
boy stayed there fifteen minutes, and running
back to the house in a state of intoxicated
delight went up to Samantha, and laying an
insistent hand on hers, said excitedly, "Oh,
Samanthy, you did n't tell me — there is
shining water down in the garden ; not so
big as the ocean, nor so still as the harbor,
but a kind of baby river running along by
itself with the sweetest noise.   Please, Miss
Vilda, may I take Gay to see it, and will it
hurt it if I wash Rags in it ? "

"Let 'em all go," suggested Samantha ;
"there 's Jabe dawdlin' along the road, and
they might as well be out from under foot."

"Don't be too hard on Jabe this morning,
Samanthy, — he 's been to see the Baptist
minister at Edgewood ; you know he 's going
to be baptized some time next month."

"Well, he needs it !   But land sakes!
you could n't make them Slocums pious 'f
you kep' on baptizin' of 'em till the crack o'
doom.   I never hearn tell of one o' them

long-legged Slocums gittin' baptized in July.
They allers take 'em after the freshets in
the spring o' the year, 'n' then they have to
be turrible careful to douse 'em lengthways
of the river. Look at him, will ye? I b'lieve
he 's grown sence yesterday! If he 'd ever
stood stiff on his feet when he was a boy,
he need n't 'a' been so everlastin' tall; but he
was forever roostin' on fences with his laigs
danglin' till the heft of his feet stretched 'em
out, — it could n't do no dif'rent. I ain't got
no patience with him."

"Jabe has considerable many good points,"
said Miss Cummins loyally; "he 's faithful,
— you always know where to find him."

"Good reason why," retorted Samantha.
"You always know where to find him 'cause
he gen'ally hain't moved sence you seen him
last. Gittin' religion ain't goin' to help him
much. If he ever hears tell 'bout the gate
of heaven bein' open 't the last day, he won't
'a' begun to begin thinkin' 'bout gittin' in
till he hears the door shet in his face; 'n'
then he 'll set ri' down 's comf'table 's if he
was inside, 'n' say, 'Wall, better luck next
time: slow an' sure 's my motto!' — Good-
mornin', Jabe; had your dinner?"

"I ain't even hed my breakfast," responded Mr. Slocum easily.

"Blessed are the lazy folks, for they always git their chores done for 'em," remarked Samantha scathingly, as she went to the buttery for provisions.

"Wall," said Laigs, looking at her with his most irritating smile, as he sat down at the kitchen table, "I don't find I git thru any more work by tumblin' out o' bed 't sun-up 'n I dew 'f I lay a spell 'n' let the univarse git het up 'n' runnin' a leetle mite. 'Slow 'n' easy goes fur in a day''s my motto. Rhapseny, she used to say she should think I'd be ashamed to lay abed so late. 'Wall, I be,' s' I, 'but I'd ruther be ashamed 'n git up!' But you 're an awful good cook, Samanthy, if ye air allers in a hurry, 'n' if yer hev got a sharp tongue!"

"The less you say 'bout my tongue the better!" snapped Samantha.

"Right you are," answered Jabe with a good-natured grin, as he went on with his breakfast. He had a huge appetite, another grievance in Samantha's eyes. She always said "there was no need of his being so slab-

sided 'n' slack-twisted 'n' knuckle-jointed, —
that he eat enough in all conscience, but he
would n't take the trouble to find the victuals
that would fat him up 'n' fill out his bag o'
bones."

Just as Samantha's well-cooked viands began to disappear in Jabe's capacious mouth
(he always ate precise-
ly as if he were stok-
ing an engine) his eye
rested upon a strange
object by the wood-
box, and he put down
his knife and ejacu-
lated, "Well, I swan!
Now when 'n' where 'd
I see that baby-shay?
Why, 't was yesterday.
Well, I vow, them
young ones was comin'
here, was they?"

" *Well, I swan!*"

" What   young
ones?" asked Miss Vilda, exchanging aston-
tonished glances with Samantha.

"And don't begin at the book o' Genesis
'n' go clean through the Bible, 's you gen-

'ally do. Start right in on Revelations,
where you belong," put in Samantha; for to
see a man unexpectedly loaded to the muzzle
with news, and too lazy to fire it off, was
enough to try the patience of a saint; and
even David Milliken would hardly have applied that term to Samantha Ann Ripley.

"Give a feller time to think, will yer?"
expostulated Jabe, with his mouth full of pie.
"'Everything comes to him as waits' 'd be
an awful good motto for you! Where'd I
see 'em? Why, I fetched 'em as fur as the
cross-roads myself."

"Well, I never!" "I want to know!"
cried the two women in one breath.

"I picked 'em up out on the road, a little
piece this side o' the station. 'T was at the
top o' Marm Berry's hill, that's jest where
't was. The boy was trudgin' along draggin'
the baby 'n' the basket, 'n' I thought I'd
give him a lift, so s' I, 'Goin' t' the Swamp
or t' the Falls?' s' I. 'To the Falls,' s' 'e.
'Git in,' s' I, "'n' I'll give yer a ride, 'f y'
ain't in no hurry,' s' I. So in he got, 'n' the
baby tew. When I got putty near home, I
happened ter think I'd oughter gone roun'

by the tan'ry 'n' picked up the Widder Foss,
'n' so s' I, 'I ain't goin' no nearer to the
Falls ; but I guess your laigs is good for the
balance o' the way, ain't they?' s' I. 'I
guess they be!' s' 'e. Then he thanked me
's perlite 's Deacon Sawyer's first wife, 'n'
I left him 'n' his folks in the road where I
found 'em."

"Did n't you ask where he belonged nor
where he was bound?"

"'T ain't my way to waste good breath
askin' questions 't ain't none o' my bis'ness,"
replied Mr. Slocum.

"You 're right, it ain't," responded Samantha, as she slammed the milk-pans in
the sink ; "'n' it 's my hope that some time
when you get good and ready to ask somebody somethin', they 'll be in too much of a
hurry to answer you!"

"Be they any of your folks, Miss Vildy?"
asked Jabe, grinning with delight at Samantha's ill humor.

"No," she answered briefly.

"What yer cal'latin' ter do with 'em?"

"I have n't decided yet. The boy says
they have n't got any folks nor any home ;

and I suppose it 's our duty to find a place
for 'em. I don't see but we 've got to go to
the expense of takin' 'em back to the city
and puttin' 'em in some asylum."

"How 'd they happen to come here?"

"They ran away from the city yesterday,
and they liked the looks of this place; that 's
all the satisfaction we can get out of 'em, and
I dare say it 's a pack of lies."

"That boy would n't tell a lie no more 'n
a seraphim!" said Samantha tersely.

"You can't judge folks by appearances,"
answered Vilda. "But anyhow, don't talk
to the neighbors, Jabe; and if you have n't
got anything special on hand to-day, I wish
you 'd patch the roof of the summer-house
and dig us a mess of beet greens. Keep the
children with you, and see what you make
of 'em; they 're playin' in the garden now."

"All right. I 'll size 'em up the best I
ken. Mebbe it 'll hender me in my work
some, but time was made for slaves as the
molasses said when they told it to hurry up
in winter time."

Two hours later, Miss Vilda looked from
the kitchen window and saw Jabez Slocum

coming across the road from the garden.
Timothy trudged beside him, carrying the
basket of greens in one hand, the other
locked in Jabe's huge paw, his eyes up-
turned and shining with pleasure, his lips
moving as if he were chatter-
ing like a magpie. Lady Gay
was just where you might have
expected to find her, mounted
on the towering height of
Jabe's shoulder, one tiny hand
grasping his weather-beaten
straw hat, while with the other
she whisked her willing steed
with an alder switch which had
evidently been cut for that purpose by the victim himself.

Her Willing Steed

"That's the way he's sizin'
of 'em up," said Samantha,
leaning over Vilda's shoulder
with a smile. "I'll bet they've sized him
up enough sight better 'n he has them!"

Jabe left the children outside, and came
in with the basket. Putting his hat in the
wood-box and hitching up his trousers im-
pressively, he sat down on the settle.

"Them ain't no children to be wanderin' about the earth afoot 'n' alone, 'same 's Hitty went to the beach;' nor they ain't any common truck ter be put inter 'sylums 'n' poor-farms.   There 's some young ones that 's so everlastin' chuckle-headed 'n' hombly 'n' contrairy that they ain't hardly wuth savin'; but these ain't that kind.   The baby, now you 've got her cleaned up, is han'somer 'n any baby on the river, 'n' a reg'lar chunk o' sunshine besides; I 'd be willin' ter pay her a little suthin' for livin' alongside.   The boy — well, the boy is a extra-ordinary boy.   We got on tergether 's slick as if we was twins.   That boy 's got idees, that 's what he 's got; 'n' he 's likely to grow up into — well, 'most anything."

"If you think so highly of 'em, why don't you adopt 'em?" asked Miss Vilda curtly. "That 's what they seem to think folks ought to do."

"I ain't sure but I shall," Mr. Slocum responded unexpectedly.   "If you can't find a better home for 'em somewheres, I ain't sure but I 'll take 'em myself.   Land sakes! if Rhapseny was alive I 'd adopt 'em quicker

'n blazes ; but marm won't take to the idee
very strong, I don't s'pose, 'n' she ain't much
on bringin' up children, as I ken testify.
Still, she's a heap better 'n a brick asylum
with a six-foot stone wall round it, when yer
come to that. But I b'lieve we ken do better
for 'em. I can say to folks, ' See here : here's
a couple o' smart, han'some children. You
can have 'em for nothin', 'n' need n't resk
the onsartainty o' gittin' married 'n' raisin'
yer own ; 'n' when yer come ter that, yer
would n't stan' no charnce o' gittin' any as
likely as these air, if ye did.'"

"That's true as the gospel!" said Samantha. It nearly killed her to agree with him,
but the words were fairly wrung from her
unwilling lips by his eloquence and wisdom.

"Well, we'll see what we can do for 'em,"
said Vilda in a non-committal tone ; "and
here they'll have to stay, for all I see, tell we
can get time to turn round and look 'em up
a place."

"And the way their edjercation has been
left be," continued Mr. Slocum, "is a burnin'
shame in a Christian country. I don' b'lieve
they ever see the inside of a schoolhouse !

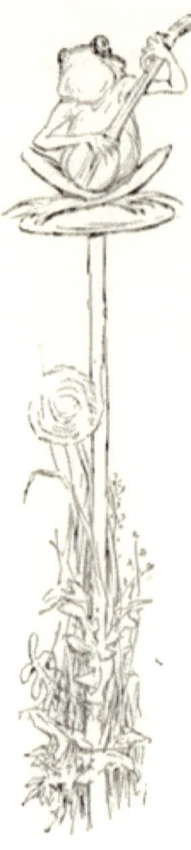

I 've learned 'em more this mornin'
'n they ever hearn tell of before,
but they 're 's ignorant 's Cooper's
cow yit, spite o' what I 've done
for 'em. They don' know tansy
from sorrel, nor slip'ry ellum from
pennyroyal, nor burdock from pig-
weed ; they don' know a dand'lion
from a hole in the ground ; they
don' know where the birds put up
when it comes on night; they
never see a brook afore, nor a
bull-frog ; they never hearn tell o'
cat-o'-nine-tails, nor jack-lanterns,
nor see-saws. Land sakes ! We
got ter talkin' 'bout so many things
that I clean forgot the summer-
house roof. But there ! this won't
do for me, I must be goin'; there
ain't no rest for the workin'-man
in this country."

"If there wan't no work for him, he 'd be
wuss off yet," responded Samantha.

"Right ye are, Samanthy ! Look here,
when 'd you want that box you give me to
fix ? "

"I wanted it before hayin', but I s'pose any time before Thanksgivin' 'll do, seein' it's you."

"What 's wuth doin' 't all 's wuth takin' time over, 's my motto," said Jabe cheerfully, "but seein' it 's you, I 'll wrassle round 'n' nail that cover on ter night or bust!"

SCENE IX

A VILLAGE SABBATH

*"Now the End of the Commandment is Charity, out of
a Pure Heart"*

I T was Sunday morning, and the very peace of God was brooding over Pleasant River. Timothy, Rags, and Gay were playing decorously in the orchard. Maria was hitched to an apple-tree in the side yard, and stood there serenely with her eyes half closed, dreaming of oats past and oats to come. Miss Vilda and Samantha issued from the mosquito-netting door, clad in Sunday best; and the children approached nearer, that they might share in the excitement of the departure for "meeting." Gay, who clamored to go, — entirely on general principles, as she had not the slightest desire for spiritual instruction, being decidedly of the earth, earthy, — was pacified by the gift of a rag doll that Samantha had made for her the evening before. It was a monstrosity, but Gay dipped it instantly in the alembic of her imagination and it became a beautiful, responsive little daughter, which she clasped close in her arms, and on which she showered the tenderest tokens of maternal affection.

Miss Vilda handed Timothy a little green paper-covered book, before she climbed into the buggy. "That's a catechism," she said; "and if you'll be a good boy and learn the first six pages and say 'em to me this afternoon, Samantha'll give you a top that you can spin on week days."

"What is a catechism?" asked Timothy, as he took the book.

"It's a Sunday-school lesson."

"Oh, then I can learn it," said Timothy, brightening; "I learned three for Miss Dora, in the city."

"Well, I'm thankful to hear that you've had some spiritual advantages; now, stay right here in the orchard till Jabe comes; and don't set the house afire," she added, as Samantha took the reins and raised them for the mighty slap on Maria's back which was necessary to wake her from her Sunday slumber.

"Why would I want to set the house afire?" Timothy asked wonderingly.

"Well, I don't know 's you would want to, but I thought you might get to playin' with matches, though I've hid 'em all."

"Play with matches!" exclaimed Timothy, in wide-eyed astonishment that a match could appeal to anybody as a desirable plaything. "Oh no, thank you; I shouldn't have thought of it."

"I wish I hadn't suggested it then; I declare, I don't know as we ought to have left 'em alone," said Vilda, looking back, as Samantha urged the moderate Maria over the road; "though I don't know exactly what they could do."

"Except run away," said Samantha reflectively.

"I wish to the land they would! It would be the easiest way out of a troublesome matter. Every day that goes by will make it harder for us to decide what to do with 'em, for you can't do by those you know the same as if they were strangers."

There was a long main street running through the village north and south. Toward the north it led through a sweet-scented wood, where the grass tufts grew in verdant

strips along the little traveled road. The
morning had been damp, though now the sun
was shining brilliantly. The spiders' webs
still covered the fields, gossamer laces of
moist, spun silver, through which shone the
pink and lilac of the meadow grasses. The
wood was a quiet place, and more than once
Miss Vilda and Samantha had discussed matters there which they would never have men-
tioned at the White Farm.

Maria went ambling along serenely through
the arcade of trees, where the sun went wandering softly, "as with his hands before his
eyes;" overhead, the vast blue canopy of
heaven; under the trees, the soft brown leaf
carpet, "woven by a thousand autumns."

"I don't know but I could grow to like
the baby in time," said Vilda, "though it's
my opinion she's goin' to be dreadful troublesome; but I'm more 'n half afraid of the
boy. Every time he looks at me with those
searchin' eyes of his, I mistrust he's goin'
to say something about Marthy, — all on account of his giving me such a turn when he
came to the door."

"He'd be awful handy round the house,

though, Vildy; that is, if he *is* handy, — pickin' up chips, 'n' layin' fires, 'n' what not; but, 's you say, he ain't so takin' as the baby at first sight. She's got the same winnin' way with her that Marthy hed!"

"Yes," said Miss Vilda grimly; "and I guess it's the devil's own way."

"Well, yes, mebbe; 'n' then again mebbe 't ain't. There ain't no reason why the devil should own all the han'some faces 'n' tunesome laughs, 't I know of. It doos seem 's if beauty was turrible misleadin', 'n' I've be'n glad

Beginning to soften a little

sometimes the Lord did n't resk none of it on me, for I was behind the door when good looks was give out, 'n' I 'm willin' t' own up to it; but, all the same, I like to see putty faces roun' me, 'n' I guess when the Lord sets his mind on it He can make goodness 'n' beauty git along comf'tably in the same body. When yer come to that, hombly folks ain't allers as good 's they might be, 'n' no comfort to anybody's eyes, nuther."

"You think the boy's all right in the upper story, do you? He's a strange kind of a child, to my thinkin'."

"I ain't so sure but he's smarter'n we be, but he talks queer, 'n' no mistake. This mornin' he was pullin' the husks off a young ear o' corn that Jabe brought in, 'n' s' 'e, 'S'manthy, I think the corn must be the happiest of all the veg'tables.' 'How you talk!' s' I; 'what makes you think that way?' 'Why, because,' s' 'e, 'God has hidden it away so safe, with all that shinin' silk round it first, 'n' then the soft leaves wrapped outside o' the silk. I guess it's God's fav'rite veg'table; don't you, S'manthy?' s' 'e. And when I was showin' him pictures last night, 'n' he see the crosses on top some o' the city meetin'-houses, s' 'e, 'They have two sticks on 'most all the churches, don't they, S'manthy? I s'pose that's one stick for God, and the other for the people.' Well, now, don't you remember Seth Pennell, o' Buttertown, how queer he was when he was a boy? We thought he'd never be wuth his salt. He used to stan' in the front winder 'n' twirl the curtin' tossel for hours to a time. And don't

you know it come out last year that he 'd
wrote a reg'lar book, with covers on it 'n'
all, 'n' that he got five dollars a colume for
writin' poetry verses for the papers?"

"Oh, well, if you mean that," said Vilda
argumentatively, "I don't call writin' poetry
any great test of smartness. There ain't
been a big fool in this village for years but
could do somethin' in the writin' line. I
guess it ain't any great trick, if you have a
mind to put yourself down to it. For my
part, I've always despised to see a great,
hulkin' man, that could handle a hoe or a
pitchfork, sit down and twirl a pen-stalk."

"Well, I ain't so sure.
I guess the Lord hes
his own way o' managin'
things. We ain't all
cal'lated to hoe perta-
ters nor yet to write po-
etry verses. There's as

Apropos of Poets

much dif'rence in folks 's there is in anybody.
Now, I can take care of a dairy as well as the
next one, 'n' nobody was ever hearn to com-
plain o' my butter; but there was that lady in
New York State that used to make flowers

'n' fruit 'n' graven images out o' her churnin's.
You 've hearn tell o' that piece she carried
to the Centennial? Now, no sech doin's 's
that ever come into my head. I 've went
on makin' round balls for twenty years ; 'n',
massy on us, don't I remember when my old
butter stamp cracked, 'n' I could n't get
another with an ear o' corn on it, 'n' hed
to take one with a beehive, why, I was that
homesick I could n't bear to look my butter
'n the eye! But that woman would have
had a new picter on her balls every day,
I should n't wonder! (For massy's sake,
Maria, don't stan' stock-still 'n' let the flies
eat yer right up!) No, I tell yer, it takes
all kinds o' folks to make a world. Now, I
could n't never read poetry. It 's so dull, it
makes me feel 's if I 'd been trottin' all day
in the sun, but there 's folks that can stan'
it, or they would n't keep on turnin' of it
out. The children are nice children enough,
but have they got any folks anywhere, 'n'
what kind of folks, 'n' where 'd they come
from, anyhow ; that 's what we 've got to find
out, 'n' I guess it 'll be consid'able of a
chore!"

"I don't know but you're right. I thought some of sendin' Jabe to the city to-morrow."

"Jabe? Well, I s'pose he'd be back by 'nother spring; but who'd we get ter shovel us out this winter, seein' as there ain't more 'n three men in the whole village? Aunt Hitty says twenty-year engagements 's goin' out o' fashion in the big cities, 'n' I'm glad if they be. They'd 'a' never come *in*, I told her, if there'd ever been an extry man in these parts, but there never was. If you got holt o' one by good luck, you had ter *keep* holt, if 't was two years or twenty-two, or go without. I used ter be too proud ter go without; now I've got more sense, thanks be! Why don't you go to the city yourself, Vildy? Jabe Slocum ain't got sprawl enough to find out anythin' wuth knowin'."

"I suppose I could go, though I don't like the prospect of it very much. I haven't been there for years, but I'd ought to look after my property there once in a while. Deary me! it seems as if we weren't ever going to have any more peace."

"Mebbe we ain't," said Samantha, as they wound up the meeting-house hill; "but ain't we hed 'bout enough peace for one spell? If peace was the best thing we could get in this world, we might as well be them old cows by the side o' the road there. There ain't nothin' so peaceful as a cow, when you come to that!"

The two women went into the church more perplexed in mind than they would have cared to confess. During the long prayer (the minister could talk to God at much greater length than he could talk about Him), Miss Vilda prayed that the Lord would provide the two little wanderers with some more suitable abiding-place than the White Farm; and that, failing this, He would inform his servant whether there was anything unchristian in sending them to a comfortable public asylum. She then reminded Heaven that she had made the Foreign Missionary Society her residuary legatee, a deed that established her claim to being a zealous member of the fold, so that she could scarcely be blamed for not wishing to take two orphan children into her peaceful home.

Well, it is no great wonder that so faulty a prayer did not bring the wished-for light at

once; but the ministering
angels, who had the fatherless little ones in their care,
did not allow Miss Vilda's
mind to rest quietly. Just as
the congregation settled itself after the hymn, and the

palm-leaf fans began to sway in the air, a
swallow flew in through the open window;
and, after fluttering to and fro over the pulpit, hid itself in a dark corner, unnoticed by
all save the small boys of the congregation,
to whom it was, of course, a priceless boon.
Miss Vilda could not keep her wandering
thoughts on the sermon any more than if
she had been a small boy. She was anything
but superstitious; but she had seen that
swallow, or some of its ancestors, before.
. . . It had flown into the church on the
very Sunday of her mother's death. . . .
They had left her sitting in the high-backed
rocker by the window, the great family
Bible and her spectacles on the little light-
stand beside her. . . . When they returned
from church, they had found their mother
sitting as they left her, with a smile on

her face, but silent and lifeless. . . . And through the glass of the spectacles, as they lay on the printed page, Vilda had read the words, "For a bird of the air shall carry the voice, and that which hath wings shall tell the matter;" had read them wonderingly, and marked the place with reverent fingers. . . . The swallow flew in again, years afterward. . . . She could not remember the day or the month, but she could never forget the summer, for it was the last bright one of her life, the last that pretty Martha ever spent at the White Farm. . . . And now here was the swallow again. . . . "For a bird of the air shall carry the voice, and that which hath wings shall tell the matter." Miss Vilda looked on the book and tried to follow the hymn; but passages of Scripture flocked into her head in place of good Dr. Watts's verses, and when the little melodeon played the interludes she could only hear: —

"Yea, the sparrow hath found her an house and the swallow a nest where she may lay her young, even Thy altars, O Lord of hosts, my King and my God."

"As a bird that wandereth from her nest, so is a man that wandereth from his place."

"The foxes have holes and the birds of the air have nests, but the Son of Man hath not where to lay his head."

And then the text fell on her bewildered ears, and roused her from one reverie to plunge her in another. It was chosen, as it chanced, from the First Epistle of Timothy, chapter first, verse fifth : "Now the end of the commandment is charity, out of a pure heart."

"That means the Missionary Society," said Miss Vilda to her conscience doggedly; but she knew better. The parson, the text, — or was it the bird? — had brought the message; but for the moment she did not lend the hearing ear or the understanding heart.

SCENE X

THE SUPPER TABLE

*Aunt Hitty comes to " make over," and supplies
Back Numbers to all the Village Histories*

AUNT HITTY, otherwise Mrs. Silas Tarbox, was as cheery and loquacious a person as you could find in a Sabbath day's journey. She was armed with a substantial amount of knowledge at almost every conceivable point; but if an unexpected emergency ever did arise, her imagination was equal to the strain put upon it and rose superior to the occasion. Yet of an evening, or on Sunday, she was no village gossip; it was only when you put a needle in her hand or a cutting-board in her lap that her memory started on its interminable journeyings through the fields of the past. She knew every biography and every "ought-to-be-ography" in the county, and could tell you the branches of every genealogical tree in the village.

It was dusk at the White Farm, and a late

supper was spread upon the hospitable board. Aunt Hitty was always sure of a bountiful repast. If one were going to economize one would not choose for that purpose the day when the village seamstress came to sew; especially when the aforesaid lady served the community in the stead of a local newspaper.

The children had eaten their bread and milk, and were out in the barn with Jabe, watching the milking. Aunt Hitty was in a cheerful mood as she reflected on her day's achievements. Out of Dr. Jonathan Cummins' old cape coat she had carved a pair of brief trousers and a vest for Timothy; out of Mrs. Jonathan Cummins' waterproof, a serviceable jacket; and out of Deacon Abijah Cummins' linen duster an additional coat and vest for warm days. The owners of these garments had been dead many years, but nothing was ever thrown away, and, for that matter, very little given away, at the White Farm, and the ancient habiliments had finally been diverted to a useful purpose.

"I hope I shall relish my vittles to-night," said Aunt Hitty, as she poured her tea into

her saucer, and set the cup in her little blue
"cup plate;" "but I 've had the neuralgy so
in my face that it 's be'n more 'n ten days
sence I 've be'n able to carry a knife to my
mouth. . . . Your meat vittles is always so
tasty, Miss Cummins. I was sayin' to Mis
Sawyer last week I think she lets her beef
hang too long. It 's dretful tender, but I
don't b'lieve its hullsome. For my part, as
I 've many a time said to Si, I like meat with
some chaw to it. Mis Sawyer don't put half
enough vittles on her table. She thinks it
scares folks; it don't me a mite, it makes
me 's hungry as a wolf. When I set a table
for comp'ny I pile on a hull lot, 'n' I find
it kind o' discourages 'em. . . . Mis Southwick 's hevin' a reg'lar brash o' house-
cleanin'. She 's too p'ison neat for any
earthly use, that woman is. She 's fixed
clam-shell borders roun' all her garding beds,
an' got enough left for a pile in one corner,
where she 's goin' to set her oleander kag.
Then she 's bought a haircloth chair and got
a new three-ply carpet in her parlor, 'n' put
the old one in the spare-room 'n' the back-
entry. Her daughter 's down here from

New Haven. She 's married into one of the
first families o' Connecticut, Lobelia has, 'n'
she puts on a good many airs. She 's rigged
out her mother's parlor with lace curtains 'n'
one thing 'n' 'other, 'n' wants it called the
drawin'-room. Did ye ever hear tell such
foolishness? 'Drawin'-room!' s' I to Si;
'what 's it goin' to draw? Nothin' but flies,
I guess likely!' (No more, thank you, my
cup ain't out yet.) Mis Pennell 's got a new
girl to help round the house, — one o' them
pindlin' light-complected Smith girls, from
the Swamp, — look 's if they was nussed
on bonny-clabber. She 's so hombly I sh'd
think 't would make her back ache to carry
her head round. She ain't very smart,
neither. Her mother sent word she 'd pick
up 'n' do better when she got her growth.
That made Mis Pennell hoppin' mad. She
said she did n't cal'late to pay a girl three
shillin's a week for growin'. Mis Pennell 's
be'n feelin' consid'able slim, or she would n't
'a' hired help; it 's just like pullin' teeth for
Deacon Pennell to pay out money for anything like that. He watches every mouthful
the girl puts into her mouth, 'n' it 's made

him 'bout down sick to see her fleshin' up
on his vittles.   They say he has her put the
mornin' coffee-groun's to dry on the winder-
sill, 'n' then has 'em scalt over for dinner;
but,   there!   I   don't
know 's there 's a mite o'
truth in it, so I won't re-
peat it.   They went to
him to git a subscription
for the new hearse the
other day.   Land sakes!
we need one bad enough.
I thought for sure, at
the last funeral we had,
that   they 'd   never git
Mis Strout to the grave-
yard safe and sound.   I

Gossip

kep' a-thinkin' all the way how she 'd 'a'
took on, if she 'd be'n alive.   She was the
most timersome woman 't ever was.   She was
a Thomson, 'n' all the Thomsons was scairt
at their own shadders.   Ivory Strout rid
right behind the hearse, 'n' he says his heart
was in his mouth the hull durin' time for
fear 't would break down 'n' spill poor Ann
Elizy out.   He did n't git much comfort out

the occasion, I guess! Wan't he mad he hed
to ride in the same buggy with his mother-
in-law! The minister planned it all out, 'n'
wrote down the order o' the mourners, 'n'
passeled him out with old Mis Thomson. I
was stan'in' close by, 'n' I heard him say he
s'posed he could go that way if he must, but
't would spile the hull blamed thing for him!
. . . Well, as I was sayin', the *seleckmen*
went to Deacon Pennell to get a contribution
towards buyin' the new hearse; an' do you
know, he would n't give 'em a dollar? He
told 'em he give five dollars towards the
other one more 'n twenty years ago, 'n'
had n't never got a cent's worth o' use out of
it. That's Deacon Pennell all over! As Si
says, if the grace o' God wan't given to all
of us without money 'n' without price, you
would n't never hev ketched Deacon Pennell
experiencin' religion! He puts an awful
sight of energy into it when he sings 'I 'm
glad salvation 's free!' and it would have to
be a free gospel that would convict him o' sin,
that 's certain! . . . They say Seth Thatcher
's married out in Iowy. His mother 's tickled
'most to death. She heerd he was settin'

up with a girl out there, 'n' she was scairt to
death for fear he'd get served as Lemuel 'n'
Cyrus was. The Thatcher boys never hed
any luck gettin' married, 'n' they always took
disappointments in love turrible hard. You
know Cyrus set in that front winder o' Mis
Thatcher's, 'n' rocked back 'n' forth for ten
year, till he wore out five cane-bottomed
cheers, 'n' then rocked clean through down
cellar all on account o' Crany Ann Sweat.
Well, I hope she got her comeuppance in
another world, — she never did in this; she
married well 'n' lived in Boston. . . . Mis
Thatcher hopes Seth 'll come home to live.
She's dretful lonesome in that big house, all
alone. She'd oughter have somebody for a
company-keeper. She can't see nothin' but
trees 'n' cows from her winders. . . . Beats
all, the places they used to put houses.
Either they'd get 'em right under foot so 't
you'd most tread on 'em when you walked
along the road, or else they'd set 'em clean
back in a lane, where the women folks
could n't see face o' clay week in 'n' week
out. (A few more o' your cold string beans,
Miss Cummins.)

"Joel Whitten's widder's just drawed his
pension along o' his bein' in the war o' 1812.
It's took 'em all these years to fix it. Massy
sakes! don't some folks have their luck but-
tered in this world? . . . She was his fourth
wife, 'n' she never lived with him but thirteen days 'fore he up 'n' died. . . . It doos
seem 's if the guv'ment might look after
things a little mite closer. . . . Talk about
Joel Whitten's bein' in the war o' 1812!
Everybody knows Joel Whitten would n't
have fit a skeeter! He never got any
further 'n Scratch Corner, anyway, 'n' there
he clim a tree or hid behind a hen-coop somewheres till the regiment got out o' sight. . . .
Yes: one, two, three, four, — Huldy was his
fourth wife. His first was a Hogg, from
Hoggses Mills. The second was Dorcas
Doolittle, aunt to Jabe Slocum; she did n't
hardly know enough to make soap, Dorcas
did n't. . . . Then there was Delia Weeks,
from the Lower Corner. . . . She did n't
live long. . . . There was somethin' wrong
with Delia. . . . She was one o' the thin-
blooded, white-livered kind. . . . You could n't
get her warm, no matter how hard you tried.

. . . She 'd set over a roarin' fire in the cook-stove even in the prickliest o' the dog-days. . . . The mill-folks used to say the Whittens burnt more cut-roun's 'n' stickens 'n any three fam'lies in the village. . . . Well, after Delia died, then come Huldy's turn, 'n' it's she, after all, that's drawed the pension. . . . Huldy took Joel's death consid'able hard, seein' as she never had him but thirteen days, but I guess she 'll perk up, now she 's come int' this money. . . . She 's awful leaky - minded, Huldy is, but she 's got tender feelin's. . . . One day she happened in at noon-time, 'n' set down to the table with Si 'n' I. . . . All of a suddent she bust right out cryin' when Si was offerin' her a piece o' tripe, 'n' then it come out that she could n't never bear the sight o' tripe, it reminded her so of Joel! It seems tripe was a favorite dish o' Joel's. All his wives cooked it first-rate. (Don't you

The Ticker

trouble to give me another plate, Samanthy.
I 've eat pretty close and I can take my pie
right on this one 'n' save washin' now you 've
got such a big family.)

"Jabe Slocum seems to set consid'able
store by them children, don't he? . . . I
guess he 'll never ketch up with his work,
now he 's got them hangin' to his heels. . . .
He doos beat all for slowness! *Slo*cum 's a
good name for him, that 's certain.   An' 's if
that wan't enough, his mother was a Still-
well, 'n' her mother was a Doolittle! . . .
The Doolittles was the slowest fam'ly in Lin-
coln County.   (Thank you, I 'm well helped,
Samanthy.)   Old Cyrus Doolittle was slower
'n a toad funeral.   He was a carpenter by
trade, 'n' he was twenty-five years buildin' his
house, 'n' it warn't no great, either. . . .
The stagin' was up ten or fifteen years, 'n' he
shingled it four or five times before he got
roun', for one patch o' shingles used to wear
out 'fore he got the next patch on.   He 'n'
Mis Doolittle lived in two rooms in the L.
There was elegant banisters, but no stairs
to 'em, 'n' no entry floors.   There was a tip-
top cellar, but there wa'n't no way o' gittin'

down to it, 'n' there wan't no conductors
to the cisterns. There was only one door
panel painted in the parlor. Land sakes!
the neighbors used to happen in 'bout every
week for years 'n' years, hopin' he 'd get another one finished up, but he never did, —
not to my knowledge. . . . Why, it 's the
gospel truth that when Mis Doolittle died he
had to have her embalmed, so 't he could git
the front door hung for the fun'ral! It was
pretty expensive, but money wan't so much
importance to Mr. Doolittle if he could save
himself hurryin'. (No more tea, I thank you.)
. . . Speakin' o' slow folks, Elder Banks tells
an awful good story 'bout Jabe Slocum. . . .
There 's another man down to Edgewood,
Aaron Peck by name, that 's 'bout as lazy as
Jabe. An' one day, when the loafers roun'
the store was talkin' 'bout 'em, all of a suddent they see the two of 'em startin' to come
down Marm Berry's hill, right in plain sight
of the store. . . . Well, one o' the Edgewood
boys bate one o' the Pleasant River boys
that they could tell which one of 'em was the
laziest by the way they come down that hill.
. . . So they all watched, 'n' bime by, when

Jabe was most down to the bottom of the
hill, they was struck all of a heap to see him
break into a kind of a jog trot 'n' run down
the balance o' the way.   Well, then, they fell
to quarrelin'; for o' course the Pleasant River

folks said Aaron Peck was the
laziest, 'n' the Edgewood boys
declared he hed n't got no such
record for laziness 's Jabe Slocum hed; an' when they was
explainin' of it, one way 'n'
'nother, Elder Banks come
along, 'n' they asked him to be
the judge.   When he heerd tell
how 't was, he said he agreed
with the Edgewood folks that
Jabe was lazier 'n Aaron.

" Could n't eat another
mossel "

'Well I snum, I don't see how
you make that out,' says the
Pleasant River boys; 'for Aaron walked
down, 'n' Jabe run a piece o' the way, 't any
rate?'   'If Jabe Slocum run,' says the Elder,
as impressive as if he was preachin', — 'if
Jabe Slocum ever run, then 't was because
he was *too doggoned lazy to hold back!*' an'
that settled it! . . . No, I could n't eat

another mossel, Miss Cummins; I 've made
out a splendid supper. . . . You can't git
such pie 'n' doughnuts anywhere else in the
village, 'n' what I say I mean. . . . Do you
make your riz doughnuts with emptin's? I
want to know! Si says there 's more faculty
in cookin' flour food than there is in meat
victuals, 'n' I guess he 's 'bout right."

. . . .

It was bed-time, and Timothy was in his
little room carrying on the most elaborate
and complicated plots for reading the future.
It must be known that Jabe Slocum was as
full of signs as a Farmer's Almanac, and he
had given Timothy more than one formula
for attaining his secret desires, — old, well-
worn recipes for luck, which had been tried
for generations in Pleasant River, and which
were absolutely certain in their results. The
favorites were : —

> " Star bright, star light,
> First star I 've seen to-night,
> Wish I may, wish I might,
> Get the wish I wish to-night ; "

and one still more impressive : —

> " Four posts upon my bed,
> Four corners overhead ;

Matthew, Mark, Luke, and John,
Bless the bed I *lay* upon.
Matthew, John, Luke, and Mark,
Grant my wish and keep it dark."

These rhymes had been chanted with great
solemnity, and Timothy sat by the open window in the sweet darkness of the summer
night, wishing that he and Gay might stay
forever in this sheltered spot. "I'll make
a sign of my very own," he thought. "I'll
get Gay's ankle-tie, and put it on the window-sill, with the toe pointing out. Then
I'll wish that if we are going to stay at the
White Farm, the angels will turn it around,
'toe in' to the room, for a sign to me;
and if we've got to go, I'll wish they may
leave it the other way; and, oh dear, but
I'm glad it's so little and easy to move;
then I'll say Matthew, Mark, Luke, and
John, four times over, without stopping, as
Jabe told me to, then I'll say my prayer
and what I can remember of the catechism,
then I'll see how it turns out in the
morning." . . .

But the incantation was more soothing
than the breath of Miss Vilda's scarlet pop-

pies, and before the magical verse had fallen upon the drowsy air for the third time, Timothy was fast asleep, with a smile of hope on his parted lips.

There was a sweet summer shower in the night. The soft breezes, fresh from shaded dells and nooks of fern, fragrant with the odor of pine and vine and wet wood-violets, blew over the thirsty meadows and golden stubble-fields, and brought an hour of gentle rain.

It sounded a merry tintinnabulation on Samantha's milk-pans, wafted the scent of dripping honeysuckle into the farmhouse windows, and drenched the night-caps in which prudent farmers had dressed their haycocks.

Next morning the green world stood on tiptoe to welcome the victorious sun, and every little leaf shone as a child's eyes might shine at the remembrance of a joy just past.

A bobolink, perched on a swaying apple-branch above Martha's grave, poured out his soul in grateful melody. Timothy, wakened by Nature's sweet good-morning, leaped from the too fond embrace of Miss Vilda's feather-bed, and lo, a miracle! Timothy's angels had interpreted his signs in their own way. The woodbine clung close to the wall beneath his window. It was tipped with strong young shoots reaching out their innocent hands to cling to any support that offered; and one baby tendril that seemed to have grown in a single night, so delicate it was, had somehow been blown by the sweet night wind from its drooping place on the parent vine, and, falling on the window-sill, had curled lovingly round Gay's fairy shoe and held it fast !

SCENE XI

THE HONEYSUCKLE PORCH

Miss Vilda decides that Two is One too many, and Timothy breaks a Humming-Bird's Egg

I T was a drowsy afternoon. The grasshoppers chirped lazily in the warm grasses, and the toads blinked sleepily under the shadows of the steps, scarcely snapping at the flies as they danced by on silver wings. Down in the old garden the still pools, in which the laughing brook rested itself here and there, shone like glass under the strong beams of the sun, and the baby horned-pouts, rustling their whiskers drowsily, scarcely stirred the water as they glided slowly through its crystal depths.

The air was fragrant with the odor of new-mown grass and the breath of wild strawberries that had fallen under the sickle to make the sweet hay sweeter with their crimson juices. The whir of the scythes and the clatter of the mowing-machine came from the distant meadows. Field mice and

ground sparrows were aware that it probably was all up with their little summer residences, for haying time was at its height, and the Giant, mounted on the Avenging Chariot, would speedily make his appearance; buttercups and daisies, tufted grasses and blossoming weeds, must all bow their heads before him, and if there was anything more valuable hidden at their roots, so much the worse!

Supposing a bird or mouse had been especially far-sighted and had located his family near a stump fence on a particularly uneven bit of ground, why there was always a walking Giant going about the edges with a gleaming scythe, so that it was no wonder, when reflecting on these matters after a day's palpitation, that the little denizens of the fields thought it very natural that there should be Nihilists and Socialists in

the world, plotting to
overturn monopolies
and other gigantic
schemes for crushing
the people.

Rags enjoyed the
excitement of haying
immensely. His life
was one long holiday
now, and the close
quarters, scanty fare,
and wearisome mo-
notony of Minerva
Court only visited his
memory dimly when
he was suffering the
pangs of indigestion.
In the first few weeks
of his life at the White Farm, before his
appetite was satiated, he was wont to eat all
the white cat's food as well as his own ; and
as this highway robbery took place in the re-
tirement of the shed, where Samantha Ann
always swept them for their meals, no human
being was any the wiser, and only the angels
saw the white cat getting whiter and whiter

and thinner and thinner, while every day
Rags grew more corpulent and aldermanic
in his figure; although as his stomach was
more favorably located than an alderman's,
he could still see the surrounding country,
and he had the further advantage of pos-
sessing four legs, instead of two, to carry it
about.

Timothy was happy, for he was a dreamer,
and this quiet life harmonized well with the
airy fabric of his dreams. He loved every
stick and stone about the old homestead
already, because the place had brought him
the only glimpse of freedom and joy that he
could remember in these last bare and anxious years; and if there were other and
brighter years, far, far back in the misty gardens of the past, they only yielded him a secret sense of "having been," a memory that
could never be captured and put into words.

Each morning he woke fearing to find his
present life a vision, and each morning he
gazed with unspeakable gladness at the sweet
reality that stretched itself before his eyes
as he stood for a moment at his window above
the honeysuckle porch.

There were the cucumber frames (he had helped Jabe to make them); the old summer-house in the garden (he had held the basket of nails and handed Jabe the tools when he patched the roof); the little workshop where Samantha potted her tomato plants (he had been allowed to water them twice, with fingers trembling at the thought of too little or too much for the tender things); and the grindstone where Jabe ground the scythes and told him stories as he sat and turned the wheel, while Gay sat beside them making dandelion chains. Yes, it was all there, and he was a part of it.

Timothy had all the poet's faculty of interpreting the secrets that are hidden in every-day things, and when he lay prone on the warm earth in the cornfield, deep among the "varnished crispness of the jointed stalks," the rustling of the green things growing sent thrills of joy along the sensitive currents of his being. He was busy in his room this afternoon putting little partitions in some cigar boxes, where, very soon, two or three dozen birds' eggs were to repose in fleece-lined nooks: for Jabe Slocum's collection of three summers (every egg acquired in the most honorable manner, as he explained) had all passed into Timothy's hands that very day, in consideration of various services well and conscientiously performed. What a delight it was to handle the precious bits of things, like porcelain in their daintiness! — to sort out the tender blue of the robin, the speckled beauty of the sparrow; to put the peewee's and the thrush's each in its place, with a swift throb of regret that there would have been another little soft throat bursting with a song, if some one had not taken this pretty egg. And there was, over and above all, the never-ending marvel of the one humming-bird's egg that lay like a pearl in Timothy's slender brown hand. Too tiny to be stroked like the others, only big enough to be stealthily kissed. So tiny that he must get out of bed two or three times in the night to see if it is safe. So tiny that he has horrible fears lest it should slip out or be stolen, and so he must take the box to the window and let the moonlight shine upon the fleecy cotton, and find that it is still there, and cover it safely over again and creep back to bed, wishing that he might see a "thumb's bigness of burnished plumage" sheltering it with her speck of a breast. Ah! to have a little humming-bird's egg to love, and to feel that it was his very own, was something to Timothy, as it is to all starved human hearts full of love that can find no outlet.

Miss Vilda was knitting, and Samantha was shelling peas on the honeysuckle porch. Several days had passed since Miss Cummins had gone to the city and come back no wiser than she went, save that she had made a somewhat exhaustive study of the slums, and had acquired a more intimate knowledge of the ways of the world than she had ever possessed before. She had found Minerva Court, and designated it on her return as a "sink of iniquity," to which Afric's sunny fountains, India's coral strand, and other tropical localities frequented by missionaries were virtuous in comparison.

"For you don't expect anything of black heathens," said she; "but there ain't any question in my mind about the accountability of folks livin' in a Christian country, where you can wear clothes and set up to an air-tight stove and be comfortable, to say nothin' of meetin'-houses every mile or two, and Bible Societies and Young Men's and Young Women's Christian Associations, and the gospel free to all with the exception of pew rents and contribution boxes, and those omitted when it 's necessary."

She affirmed that the ladies and gentlemen whose acquaintance she had made in Minerva Court were, without exception, a "mess o' malefactors," whose only good point was that, lacking all human qualities, they did not care who she was, nor where she came from, nor what she came for; so that, as a matter of fact, she had escaped without so much as leaving her name and place of residence. She learned that Mrs. Nancy Simmons had sought pastures new in Montana; that Miss Ethel Montmorency still resided in the metropolis, but did not choose to disclose her modest dwelling-place to the casual inquiring female from the rural districts; that a couple of children had disappeared from Minerva Court, if they remembered rightly, but that there was no disturbance made about the matter as it saved several people much trouble; that Mrs. Morrison had had no relations, though she possessed a large circle of admiring friends; that none of the admiring friends had called since her death or asked about the children; and finally, that Number 3 had been turned into a saloon, and she was welcome to go in and slake her thirst for information with something more satisfactory than she could get outside.

The last straw, and one that would have broken the back of any self-respecting (unmarried) camel in the universe, was the offensive belief, on the part of the Minerva Courtiers, that the rigid Puritan maiden who was conducting the examination was the erring mother of the children, visiting in disguise their former dwelling-place. The conversation on this point becoming extremely pointed and jocose, Miss Cummins finally turned and fled, escaping to the railway station as fast as her trembling legs could carry her. So the trip was a fruitless one, and the mystery that enshrouded Timothy and Lady Gay was as impenetrable as ever.

"I wish I'd 'a' gone to the city with you,"

remarked Samantha. "Not that I could 'a'
found out anything more 'n you did, for I
guess there ain't anybody thereabouts that
knows more 'n we do, and anybody 't wants
the children won't be troubled with the relation. But I 'd like to give them bold-faced
jigs 'n' hussies a good piece o' my mind for
once! You 're too timersome, Vildy! I
b'lieve I 'll go some o' these days yet, and
carry a good stout umbrella in my hand too.
It says in a book somewhars that there 's
insults that can only be wiped out in blood.
Ketch 'em hintin' that I 'm the mother of
anybody, that 's all! I declare I don' know
what our Home Missionary Societies 's doin'
not to regenerate them places or exterminate
'em, one or t' other. Somehow our religion
don't take holt as it ought to. It takes a
burnin' zeal to clean out them slum places,
and burnin' zeal ain't the style nowadays.
As my father used to say, ' Religion 's putty
much like fish 'n' pertetters; if it 's hot, it 's
good, 'n' if it 's cold 't ain't wuth a ' — well, a
short word come in there, but I won't say it.
Speakin' o' religion, I never had any experience in teachin', but I did n't s'pose there

was any knack 'bout teachin' religion, same
as there is 'bout teachin' readin' 'n' 'rithme-
tic, but I hed hard work makin' Timothy
understand that catechism you give him to
learn the other Sunday. He was all upsot
with doctrine when he come to say his lesson.
Now you can't scare some children with doctrine, no matter how hot you make it, or
mebbe they don't more 'n half believe it ; but
Timothy 's an awful sensitive creeter, 'n'
when he come to that answer to the question
'What are you then by nature? An enemy
to God, a child of Satan, and an heir of hell,'
he hid his head on my shoulder and bust
right out cryin'. 'How many Gods is there?'
s' 'e, after a spell. 'Land!' thinks I, 'I knew
he was a heathen, but if he turns out to be
an idolater, whatever shall I do with him!'
'Why, where 've you be'n fetched up?' s' I ;
there 's only one God, the High and Mighty
Ruler of the Univarse,' s' I. 'Well,' s' 'e,
'there must be more 'n one, for the God in
this lesson is n't like the one in Miss Dora's
book at all!' Land sakes! I don't want to
teach catechism agin in a hurry, not till I 've
hed a little spiritual instruction from the

minister. The fact is, Vildy, that our b'liefs, when they 're picked out o' the Bible and set down square and solid 'thout any softening down 'n' explainin' that they ain't so bad as they sound, is too strong meat for babes. Now I 'm Orthodox to the core " (here she lowered her voice as if there might be a stray deacon in the garden), " but 'pears to me if I was makin' out lessons for young ones I would n't fill 'em so plumb full o' brimstun. Let 'em do a little suthin' to deserve it 'fore you scare 'em to death, say I."

" Jabe explained it all out to him after supper. It beats all how he gets on with children."

"I 'd ruther hear how he explained it," answered Samantha sarcastically. " He 's great on expoundin' the Scripters jest now. Well, I hope it 'll last. Land sakes! you 'd think nobody ever experienced religion afore, he 's so set up 'bout it. You 'd s'pose he kep' the latch-key o' the heavenly mansions right in his vest pocket, to hear him go on. He could n't be no more stuck up 'bout it if he was the only sinner that ever repented. I notice he took plaguey good care to git

converted in the meetin'-house nearest home.
You would n't ketch him travelin' fur for
his salvation."

"There goes Elder Nichols," said Miss
Vilda. "Now there's a plan we had n't
thought of. We might take the children
over to Purity Village. I think likely the
Shakers would take 'em. They like to get
young folks and break 'em in to their doctrines."

"Tim 'd make a tip-top Shaker," laughed
Samantha. "He 'd be an Elder afore he
was twenty-one. I can seem to see him now,
with his hair danglin' long in his neck, a blue
coat buttoned up to his chin, and his hands
see-sawin' up 'n' down, prancin' round in
them solemn dances."

"Tim would do well enough, but I ain't
so sure of Gay. They 'd have their hands
full with her, I guess!"

"I guess they would. Anybody that
wanted to make a Shaker out o' her would
'a' had to begin with her grandmother; and
that would n't 'a' done nuther, for they don't
b'lieve in marryin', and the thing would 'a'
stopped right there, and Gay would n't never
'a' been born int' the world."

"And been a great sight better off," interpolated Miss Vilda.

"Now don't talk that way, Vildy. Who knows what lays ahead o' that child? The Lord may be savin' her up to do some great work for Him," she added, with a wild flight of the imagination.

"She looks like it, don't she?" asked Vilda with a grim intonation; but her face softened a little as she glanced at Gay asleep on the rustic bench under the window.

The picture would have struck terror to the sad-eyed æsthete, but an artist who liked to see colors burn and glow on the canvas would have been glad to paint her; a little frock of buttercup calico, bare dimpled neck and arms, hair that put the yellow calico to shame by reason of its tinge of copper, skin of roses and milk that dared the microscope, red smiling lips, one stocking and ankle-tie kicked off and five pink toes calling for some silly woman to say "This little pig went to market;" a great bunch of nasturtiums in one warm hand, the other buried in Rags, who was bursting with the white cat's dinner, and in such a state of snoring bliss that his tail wagged occasionally, even in his dreams.

"She don't look like a missionary at this minute, if that's what you mean," said Samantha hotly. "She may not be called 'n' elected to traipse over to Africy with a test'-ment in one hand 'n' a sun umbreller in the other, savin' souls by the wholesale; but 't ain't no mean service to go through the world stealin' into folks' hearts like

Gay asleep

a ray o' sunshine, 'n' lightin' up every place you step foot in!"

"I ain't sayin' anything against the child, Samanthy Ann; you said yourself she wan't cut out for a Shaker!"

"No more she is," laughed Samantha, when her good humor was restored. "She'd like the singin' 'n' dancin' well enough, but 't would be hard work smoothin' the kink out of her hair 'n' fixin' it under one o' their white Sunday bunnets. She would n't like livin' altogether with the women-folks nuther.

The only way for Gay 'll be to fetch her
right up with the men-folks, 'n' hev her see
they ain't no great things, anyway. Land
sakes! if 't warn't for dogs 'n' dark nights,
I should n't care if I never see a man; but
Gay has 'em all on her string a'ready, from
the boy that brings the cows home for Jabe
to the man that takes the butter to the city.
The tin peddler give her a dipper this mornin', and the fish-man brought her a live fish
in a tin pail. Well, she makes the house a
great sight brighter to live in, you can't deny
that, Vildy."

"I ain't denyin' anything in partic'ler.
She makes a good deal of work, I know that
much. And I don't want you to get your
heart set on one or both of 'em, for 't won't
be no use. We could make out with one of
'em, I suppose, if we had to, but two is one
too many. They seem to set such store
by one another that 't would be like partin'
the Siamese twins; but there, they'd pine
awhile, and then they'd get over it. Anyhow, they'll have to try."

"Oh yes; you can git over the small-pox,
but you'll carry the scars to your grave most

likely. I think 't would be a sin to part them
children. I would n't do it no more 'n I 'd
tear away that scarlit bean that 's twisted
itself round 'n' round that pink hollyhock
there. I stuck a stick in the ground, and
carried a string to the winder; but I did n't
git at it soon enough, the bean vine kep' on
growin' the other way, towards the hollyhock.
Then the other night I got my mad up, 'n'
I jest oncurled it by main force 'n' wropped
it round the string, 'n' if you 'll believe me, I
happened to look at it this mornin', 'n' there
't was, as nippant as you please, coiled round
the hollyhock agin! Then says I to myself,
'Samantha Ann Ripley, you 've known what
't was to be everlastin'ly hectored 'n' interfered with all your life, now s'posin' you let
that bean have its hollyhock, if it wants
it!'"

Miss Vilda looked at her sharply as she
said, "Samantha Ann Ripley, I believe to
my soul you 're fussin' 'bout Dave Milliken
again."

"Well, I ain't! Every time I talk 'bout
hollyhocks and scarlit beans I ain't meanin'
Dave Milliken 'n' me, — not by a long chalk!

I was only givin' you my views 'bout partin' them children, that 's all!"

"Well, all I can say is," remarked Miss Vilda obstinately, "that those that 's desirous of takin' in two strange children, and boardin' and lodgin' 'em till they get able to do it for themselves, and runnin' the resk of their turnin' out heathens and malefactors like the folks they came from, — can do it if they want to. If I come to see that the baby is too young to send away anywheres I may keep her a spell, but the boy has got to go, and that 's the end of it. You 've been crowdin' me into a corner about him for a week, and now I 've said my say!"

Alas! that tiny humming-bird's egg was crushed to atoms, — crushed by a boy's slender hand that had held it so gently for very fear of breaking it. Poor little Timothy Jessup had heard his fate for the second time, and knew that he must "move on" again, for there was no room for him at the White Farm.

SCENE XII

THE VILLAGE

Lyddy Pettigrove's Funeral

LYDDY PETTIGROVE, David Milliken's sister, was dead. Not one person, but a dozen had called in at the White Farm to announce this fact and look curiously at Samantha Ann Ripley to see how she took the news.

To say the truth, the community did not seem to be overpowered by its bereavement. There seemed to be a general feeling that Mrs. Pettigrove had never been wanted in Pleasant River, coupled with a mild surprise that she should have been welcome anywhere else, even in heaven, where she must have gone, being a church member. Speculation was rife as to who would keep house for Dave Milliken, and whether Samantha Ann would bury the Ripley-Milliken battle-axe and go to the funeral, and whether Mrs. Pettigrove had left her property to David, as was right, or to her husband's sister in New Hampshire, "which would be a sin and a shame, but jest as likely as not, though she was well off and did n't need it no more 'n a toad would a pocket-book, and could n't bear the sight o' Lyddy besides," — and whether Mr. Petti-grove's first wife's relations would be asked to the funeral, "bein' as how they had n't spoke for years, 'n' would n't set on the same side the meetin'-house, but when you come to that, if only the folks that was on good terms with Lyddy Pettigrove was asked to the funeral, there 'd be a slim attendance," and — so on.

Aunt Hitty was the most important person in the village on these occasions. It was she who assisted in the last solemn preparations and took the last solemn stitches. When all was done, she hung her little reticule on her arm, and started to walk from the house of bereavement to her own home, where "Si" was anxiously awaiting his nightly draught of gossip. No royal herald could have been looked for with greater interest or greeted with greater cordiality. All the housewives that lived on the direct

road were on their doorsteps, so as not to
lose a moment, and all that lived off the road
had seen her from the upstairs windows, and
were at the gate to waylay her as she passed.
At such a moment Aunt Hitty's bosom
swelled with honest pride, and she humbly
thanked her Maker that she had been bred
to the use of scissors and needle.

Two days of this intoxicating popularity
had just past; the funeral was over, and she
ran in to the White Farm on her way home,
to carry a message and to see with her own
eyes how Samantha Ann Ripley was comporting herself.

"You didn't git out to the fun'ral, did ye,
Samanthy?" she asked, as she seated herself cosily by the kitchen window.

"No, I didn't. I never could see the
propriety o' goin' to see folks dead that you
never went to see alive."

"How you talk! That's one way o' puttin' it! Well, everybody was lookin' for
you, and you missed a very pleasant fun'ral.
David 'n' I arranged everything as neat
as wax, and it all went off like clockwork, if
I do say so as shouldn't. Mis Pettigrove
made a beautiful remains."

"I 'm glad to hear it. It 's the first beautiful thing she ever did make, I guess!"

"How you talk! Ain't you a leetle hard on Lyddy, Samanthy? She warn't sech a bad neighbor, and she could n't help bein' kind o' sour like. She was born with her teeth on aidge, to begin with, and then she 'd be'n through seas o' trouble with them Pettigroves."

"Like enough ; but even if folks has be'n through seas o' trouble, they need n't be everlastin'ly spittin' up salt brine. 'Passin' through the valley of sorrow they make it full o' fountings ;' that 's what the Psalms says 'bout bearin' trouble."

"Lyddy warn't much on fountings," said Aunt Hitty contemplatively ; "but there, we had n't ought to speak nothin' but good o' the dead. Land sakes! You 'd oughter heard Elder

Elder Weeks

Weekses remarks ; they was splendid. We ain't hed better remarks to any fun'ral here for years. I should n't 'a' suspicioned he was preachin' 'bout Lyddy, though. Our minister 's sick abed, you know, 'n' warn't

able to conduct the ex'cises. Si thinks he
went to bed a-purpose, but I would n't hev
it repeated ; so David got Elder Weeks from
Moderation. He warn't much acquainted
with the remains, but he done all the better
for that. He's got a wond'ful faculty for
fun'rals. They say he's sent for for miles
around. He'd just come from a fun'ral
nine miles the other side o' Moderation, up
on the Blueb'ry road ; so he was a leetle
mite late, 'n' David 'n' I was as nervous as
witches, for every room was cram full 'n' the
thermometer stood at 87 in the front entry,
'n' the bearers sot out there by the well-
curb, with the sun beatin' down on 'em, 'n'
two of 'em, Squire Hicks 'n' Deacon Dunn,
was fast asleep. Inside, everything was as
silent 's the tomb, 'cept the kitchen clock,
'n' that ticked loud enough to wake the
dead most. I thought I should go inter
conniptions. I set out to git up 'n' throw a
shawl over it, it ticked so loud. Then, while
we was all settin' there 's solemn 's the last
trump, what does old Aunt Beccy Burnham
do but git up from the kitchen corner where
she sot, take the corn-broom from behind the

door, and sweep down a cobweb that was
lodged up in one o' the corners over the mantelpiece ! We all looked at one 'nother, 'n'
I thought for a second somebody'd laugh,
but nobody dassed, 'n' there warn't a sound
in the room 's Aunt Beccy sot down agin'
without movin' a muscle in her face. Just
then the minister drove in the yard with his
horse sweatin' like rain ; but behind time as
he was, he never slighted things a mite. His
prayer was twenty-three minutes by the
clock. Twenty - three minutes is a leetle
mite too long this kind o' weather, but it
was an all-embracin' prayer, 'n' no mistake !
Si said when he got through, the Lord had
his instructions on most any p'int that was
likely to come up durin' the season. When
he got through his remarks there warn't a
dry eye in the room. I don't s'pose it made
any odds whether he was preachin' 'bout
Mis Pettigrove or the woman on the Blueb'ry
road, — it was a movin', elevatin' discourse,
'n' that was what we went there for."

   " It would n't 'a' be'n so elevatin' if he'd
told the truth," said Samantha ; " but there,
I ain't goin' to spit no more spite out.

Lyddy Pettigrove's dead, 'n' I hope she's in
heaven, and all I can say is, that she'll be
dretful busy up there ondoin' all she done
down here. You say there was a good many
out ?"

"Yes ; we ain't hed so many out for years,
so Susanna Rideout says, and she'd ought to
know, for she ain't missed a fun'ral sence
she was nine years old, and she's eighty-one,
come Thanksgivin', ef she holds out that
long. She says fun'rals is 'bout the only
recreation she has, 'n' she doos git a heap
o' satisfaction out of 'em, 'n' no mistake.
She'll go early, afore any o' the comp'ny
assembles. She'll say her clock must 'a'
be'n fast, 'n' then they'll ask her to set
down 'n' make herself to home. Then she'll
choose her seat accordin' to the way the
house is planned. She won't git too fur
from the remains, because she'll want to see
how the fam'ly appear when they take their
last look, but she'll want to git opp'site a
door, where she can peek into the other
rooms 'n' see whether they shed any tears
when the minister begins his remarks. She
allers takes a little gum camphire in her

pocket, so 't if anybody faints away during the long prayer she 's right on hand. Bein' near the door, she can hear all the minister says, 'n' how the order o' the mourners is called, 'n' ef she ain't too fur from the front winders she can hev a good view of the bearers and the mourners as they get into the kerridges. There 's a sight in knowin' how to manage at a fun'ral; it takes faculty, same as anything else."

"How does David bear up?" asked Miss Vilda.

"Oh, he 's calm. David was always calm and resigned, you know. He shed tears durin' the remarks, but I s'pose, mebbe, he was wishin' they was more appropriate. He 's about the forlornest creeter now you ever see in your life. There never was any self-assume to David Milliken. I declare it 's enough to make you cry jest to look at him. I cooked up victuals enough to last him a week, but that ain't no way for menfolks to live. When he comes in at noontime he washes up out by the pump, 'n' then he steps int' the butt'ry 'n' pours some cold tea out the teapot 'n' takes a drink of it, 'n'

then a bite o' cold punkin-pie 'n' then more
tea, all the time stan'in' up to the shelf 'stid
o' sittin' down like a Christian, — and lookin'
out the winder as if his mind was in Hard
Scrabble 'n' his body in Buttertown, 'n' as if
he did n't know whether he was eatin' pie

"*The tears that blinded her eyes*"

or putty. Land! I can't bear to watch him.
I dassay he misses Lyddy's jawin'; it must
seem dretful quiet. I declare it seems to
me that meek, resigned folks, that's too
good to squeal out when they're abused, is
allers the ones that gits the hardest knocks;
but I don't doubt but what there's goin' to
be an everlastin' evenupness somewheres."

Samantha got up suddenly and went to the sink window. "It 's 'bout time the men come in for their dinner," she said ; and although Jabe was mowing the millstone hill, in a flaming red flannel shirt, she could not see him because of the tears that blinded her eyes.

SCENE XIII

THE VILLAGE

*Pleasant River is baptized with the Spirit of
Adoption*

UT I did n't come in to talk 'bout the fun'ral," continued Aunt Hitty, wishing that human flesh were transparent so that she could see through Samanthy Ann Ripley's back. "I had an errant 'n' oughter be'n in afore, but I 've been so busy these last few days I could n't find rest for the sole o' my foot skersely. I 've sewed in seven dif'rent houses sence I was here last, and I 've made it my biz'ness to try 'n' stop the gossip 'bout them children 'n' give folks the rights o' the matter, 'n' git 'em int'rested to do somethin' for 'em. Now there ain't a livin' soul that wants the boy, but " —

"Timothy," said Miss Vilda hurriedly, "run and fetch me a passle of chips, that 's a good boy. Land sakes, Aunt Hitty, you need n't tell him to his face that nobody wants him. He 's got feelin's like any other child."

" He set there so quiet with a book in front
of him I clean forgot he was in the room,"
said Aunt Hitty apologetically.   " Land !
I 'm so tender-hearted I can't set my foot on
a June bug, 'n' 't ain't likely I 'd hurt anybody's feelin's, but as I was sayin' I can't
find nobody that wants the boy, but the Doctor's wife thinks p'raps she 'll be willin' to
take the baby 'n' board her for nothin', if
somebody else 'll pay for her clothes.   At
least she 'll try her a spell 'n' see how she
behaves, 'n' whether she 's good comp'ny for
her own little girl that 's a reg'lar limb o'
Satan anyway, 'n' consid'able worse sence
she 's had the scarlit fever, 'n' deef as a post
too, tho' they 're blisterin' her, 'n' she may
git over it.   I told her I 'd bring Gay over
to-night as I was comin' by, bein' as how she
was worn out with sickness 'n' house-cleanin'
'n' one thing 'n' 'nother, 'n' could n't come to
git her very well herself.   I thought mebbe
you 'd be willin' to pay for her clothes ruther
'n hev so much talk 'bout it, tho' I 've told
everybody that they walked right in to the
front gate, 'n' you 'n' Samanthy never set
eyes on 'em before, 'n' did n't know where
they come from."

Samantha wiped her eyes surreptitiously with the dishcloth and turned a scarlet face away from the window. Timothy was getting his " passle of chips." Gay had spied him, and toddling over to his side, holding her dress above the prettiest pair of feet that ever trod clover, had sat down on him (a favorite pastime of hers), and after jolting her fat little person up and down on his patient head, rolled herself over and gave him a series of bear-hugs. Timothy looked pale and languid, Samantha thought, and though Gay waited for a frolic with her most adorable smile, he only lifted her coral necklace to kiss the place where it hung, and tied on her sun-bonnet soberly. Samantha wished that Vilda had been looking out of the window. Her own heart did not need softening, but somebody else's did, she was afraid.

"I'm much obliged to you for takin' so much interest in the children," said Miss Vilda primly, "and partic'lerly for clearin' our characters, which everybody that lives in this village has to do for each other 'bout once a week, and the rest o' the time they take for spoilin' of 'em. And the Doctor's wife is very kind, but I should n't think o' sendin' the baby away so sudden while the boy is still here. It would n't be no kindness to Mrs. Mayo, for she 'd have a reg'lar French and Indian war right on her premises. It was here the children came, just as you say, and it 's our duty to see 'em settled in good homes, but I shall take a few days more to think 'bout it, and I 'll let her know by Saturday night what we 've decided to do. — That 's the most meddlesome, interferin', gossipin' woman in this county," she added, as Mrs. Silas Tarbox closed the front gate, "and I would n't have her do another day's work at this house if I did n't have to. But it 's worse for them that don't have her than for them that does. — Now there 's the Baptist minister drivin' up to the barn. What under the canopy does he want? Tell him Jabe ain't to home, Samanthy. No, you need n't, for he 's hitched, and seems to be comin' to the front door."

"I never could abide the looks of him," said Samantha, peering over Miss Vilda's shoulder. "'T ain't his doctrines I object to so much, though bein' a good Congregation-

alist I don't see no sense in 'em, but a man
with a light chiny blue eye like that ought
not to be allowed to go int' the ministry.
You can't love your brother whom you hev
seen with that kind of an eye, and how are
you goin' to love the Lord whom you hev not
seen ?"

Mr. Southwick, who was a spare man in
a long linen duster that looked as if it had
not been in the water as often as its wearer,
sat down timidly on the settle and cleared
his throat.

"I've come to talk with you on a little
matter of business, Miss Cummins. Brother
Slocum has — a — conferred with me on the
subject of a — a — couple of unfortunate
children who have — a — strayed, as it were,
under your hospitable roof, and whom — a —
you are properly anxious to place — a — under other rooves, as it were. Now you are
aware, perhaps, that Mrs. Southwick and I
have no children living, though we have at
times had our quivers full of them — a — as
the Scripture says, but the Lord gave and
the Lord hath taken away, blessed be the
name of the Lord; however, that is — a —

neither here nor there.   Brother Slocum has
so interested us that my wife (who is leading
the Woman's Auxiliary Praying Legion this
afternoon or she would have come herself)
wishes me to say that she would like to receive one of these — a — little waifs into our
family on probation, as it were, and if satisfactory to both parties, to bring it up — a —
somewhat as our own, in the nurture and
admonition of the Lord."

Samantha waited in breathless suspense.
Miss Vilda never would fling away an oppor-
tunity of putting a nameless, homeless child
under the roof of a minister of the Gospel,
even if he was a Baptist with a chiny blue
eye.   At this exciting juncture there was a
clatter of small feet ; the door burst open, and
the "unfortunate waifs" under consideration raced across the floor to the table where
Miss Vilda and Samantha were seated.
Gay's sun-bonnet trailed behind her, every
hair on her head curled separately, and she
held her rag-doll upside down with entire
absence of decorum.   Timothy's paleness,
whatever the cause, had disappeared for the
moment, and his eyes shone like stars.

"Oh, Miss Vilda!" he cried breathlessly; "dear Miss Vilda and Samanthy, the gray hen *did* want to have chickens, and that is what made her so cross, and she is setting, and we 've found her nest in the alder bushes by the pond!"

"*We 've found her nest*"

("Gay hen's net in er buttes by er pond," sung Gay, like a Greek chorus.)

"And we sat down softly beside the pond, but Gay sat into it."

("Gay sat wite into it, an' dolly dot her dess wet, but Gay nite ittle dirl; Gay didn't det wet!")

"And by and by the gray hen got off to get a drink of water" —

("To det a dink o' water" —)

"And we counted the eggs, and there were thirteen big ones!"

("Fir-teen drate bid ones!")

"So that the darling thing had to s-w-ell out to cover them up!"

("Darlin' fin ser-welled out an' turveved 'em up!") said Gay, going through the same operation.

"Yes," said Miss Vilda, looking covertly at Mr. Southwick (who had an eye for beauty, notwithstanding Samantha's strictures), "that's very nice, but you must n't stay here now; we are talkin' to the minister. Run away, both of you, and let the settin' hen alone.—Well, as I was goin' to say, Mr. Southwick, you're very kind and so's your wife, and I'm sure Timothy, that's the boy's name, would be a great help and comfort to both of you, if you're fond of children, and we should be glad to have him near by, for we feel kind of responsible for him, though he's no relation of ours. And we'll think about the matter over night, and let you know in the morning."

"Yes, exactly, I see, I see; but it was the young child, the — a — female child, that my wife desired to take into her family. She does not care for boys, and she is particularly fond of girls, and so am I, very fond of girls — a — in reason."

Miss Vilda all at once made up her mind

on one point, and only wished that Samantha
would n't stare at her as if she had never
seen her before. " I 'm sorry to disappoint
your wife, Mr. Southwick. It seems that
Mrs. Tarbox and Jabez Slocum have been
offerin' the child to every family in the village, and I s'pose bime bye they 'll have the
politeness to offer her to me ; but, at any
rate, whether they do or not, I propose to
keep her myself, and I 'd thank you to tell
folks so, if they ask you. Mebbe you 'd
better give it out from the pulpit, though I
can let Mrs. Tarbox know, and that will answer the same purpose. This is the place
the baby was brought, and this is the place
she 's goin' to stay."

"Vildy, you 're a good woman !" cried
Samantha, when the door closed on the Reverend Mr. Southwick. " I 'm proud o' you,
Vildy, 'n' I take back all the hard thoughts
I 've be'n hevin' about you lately. The idee
o' that chiny-eyed preacher thinkin' he was
goin' to carry that child home in his buggy
with hardly so much as sayin' 'Thank you,
marm !' I like his imperdence ! His wife
hed better wash his duster afore she adopts

any children. If they 'd carry their theories 'bout immersion 's fur as their clo'es, 't would n't be no harm."

"You need n't give me any compliments. I don' know as I 'd have agreed to keep either of 'em ef the whole village had n't interfered and wanted to manage my business for me, and be so dretful charitable all of a sudden, and dictate to me and try to show me my duty. I have n't had a minute's peace for more 'n a fortnight, and now I hope they 'll let me alone. I 'll take the boy to the city to-morrow, if I live to see the light, and when I come back I 'll tie up the gate and keep the neighbors out till this nine days' wonder gets crowded out o' their heads by somethin' new."

"You 're goin' to take Timothy to the city, are you?" asked Samantha sharply.

"That's what I 'm goin' to do; and the sooner the better for everybody concerned. — Timothy, shut that door and run out to the barn, and don't you let me see you again till supper-time; do you hear me?" —

"And you 're goin' to put him in one o' them Homes?"

"Yes, I am. You see for yourself we can't find any place fer him hereabouts."

"Well, I've be'n waitin' for days to see what you was goin' to do, and now I'll tell you what I'm goin' to do, if you'd like to know. I'm goin' to keep Timothy myself; to have and to hold from this time forth and for evermore, as the Bible says. That's what I'm goin' to do!"

Miss Cummins gasped with astonishment.

"I mean what I say, Vildy. I ain't so well off as some, but I ain't a pauper, not by no means. I've be'n layin' by a little every year for twenty years, 'n' you know well enough

Hard to melt

what for; but that's all over for ever and ever, amen, thanks be! And I ain't got chick nor child, nor blood relation in the world, and if I choose to take somebody to do for, why, it's nobody's affairs but my own."

"You can't do it, and you shan't do it!"

said Miss Vilda excitedly. "You ain't goin'
to make a fool of yourself, if I can help it.
We can't have two children clutterin' up
this place and eatin' us out of house and
home, and that's the end of it."

"It ain't the end of it, Vildy Cummins,
not by no manner o' means! If we can't
keep both of 'em, do you know what I think
'bout it? I think we'd ought to give away
the one that everybody wants and keep the
other that nobody does want, more fools
they! That's religion, accordin' to my way
o' thinkin'. I love the baby, dear knows;
but see here. Who planned this thing all
out? Timothy. Who took that baby up in
his own arms and fetched her out o' that den
o' thieves? Timothy. Who stood all the
resk of gittin' that innocent lamb out o' that
sink of iniquity, and hed wit enough to bring
her to a place where she could grow up respectable? Timothy. And do you ketch
him sayin' a word 'bout himself from fust to
last? Not by no manner o' means. That
ain't Timothy. And what does the lovin'
gen'rous, faithful little soul git? He gits
his labor for his pains. He hears folks say

right to his face that nobody wants him and everybody wants Gay. And if he did n't have a disposition like a cherubim-an-seraphim (and better, too, for they 'continually do cry,' now I come to think of it), he 'd be sour and bitter 'stid o' bein' good as an angel in a picture-book from sun-up to sundown!"

Miss Vilda was crushed by the overpowering weight of this argument, and did not even try to stem the resistless tide of Samantha's eloquence.

" And now folks is all of a high to take in the baby for a spell, jest for a plaything, because her hair curls, 'n' she 's han'some, 'n' light complected, 'n' a girl (whatever that amounts to is more 'n I know !), and that blessed boy is trod under foot as if he warn't no better 'n an angle-worm ! And do you mean to tell me you don't see the Lord's hand in this hull bus'ness, Vildy Cummins? There 's other kinds o' meracles besides buddin' rods 'n' burnin' bushes 'n' loaves 'n' fishes. What do you s'pose guided that boy to pass all the other houses in this village 'n' turn in at the White Farm ? Don't you s'pose he was led ? Well, I don't need a Bible nor yit a concordance to tell *me* he was. *He* did n't know there was plenty 'n' to spare inside this gate; a great empty house 'n' full cellar, 'n' hay 'n' stock in the barn, and cowpons in the bank, 'n' two lone, mis'-able women inside, with nothin' to do but keep flies out in summer-time, 'n' pile wood on in winter-time, till they got so withered up 'n' gnarly they warn't hardly wuth geth-erin' int' the everlastin' harvest! *He* did n't know it, I say, but the Lord did; 'n' the Lord's intention was to give us a chance to make our callin' 'n' election sure, 'n' we can't do that by turnin' our backs on His messenger, and puttin' of him ou'doors! The Lord intended them children should stay together or He would n't 'a' started 'em out that ₊way; now that 's as plain as the nose on my face, 'n' that 's consid'able plain as I 've be'n told afore now, 'n' can see for myself in the glass without any help from anybody, thanks be!"

" Everybody 'll laugh at us for a couple o' soft-hearted fools," said Miss Vilda feebly, after a long pause. " We 'll be a spectacle for the whole village."

"What if we be? Let's be a spectacle, then!" said Samantha stoutly. "We'll be a spectacle for the angels as well as the village, when you come to that! When they look down 'n' see us gittin' out-side this door-yard 'n'

A Spectacle for Angels

doin' one o' the Lord's chores for the first time in ten or fifteen years, I guess they will be consid'able excited! But there's no use in talkin', I 've made up my mind, Vildy. We've lived together for thirty years 'n' ain't hardly hed an ugly word, 'n' dretful dull it hez be'n for both of us, 'n' I shan't live nowheres else without you tell me to go ; but I 've got lots o' good work in me yit, 'n' I 'm goin' to take that boy up 'n' give him a chance, 'n' let him stay alongside o' the thing he loves best in the world. And if there ain't room for all of us in the fourteen rooms o' this part o' the house, Timothy 'n' I can live in the L, as you've allers intended I should if I got married. And I guess this is 'bout as near to gittin' married as either of us ever 'll git now, 'n' consid'able nearer 'n' I 've expected to git, lately. And I 'll tell Timothy this very night, when he goes to bed, for he 's grievin' himself into a fit o' sickness, as anybody can tell that 's got a glass eye in their heads!"

SCENE XIV

A POINT OF HONOR

*Timothy Jessup runs away a Second Time, and, like
Other Blessings, brightens as He takes His Flight*

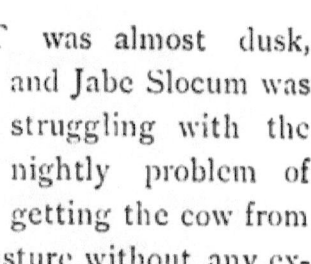

IT was almost dusk, and Jabe Slocum was struggling with the nightly problem of getting the cow from the pasture without any expenditure of personal effort. Timothy was nowhere to be found, or he would go and be glad to do the trifling service for his kind friend without other remuneration than a cordial "Thank you." Failing Timothy, there was always Billy Pennell, who would not go for a "Thank you," being a boy of a sordid and miserly manner of thought, but who would go for a cent and chalk the cent up, which made it a more reasonable charge than would appear to the casual observer. So Jabe lighted his corn-cob pipe, and extended himself under a willow-tree beside the pond, singing in a cheerful fashion, —

> "'Tremblin' sinner, calm your fears!
>   Jesus is always ready.
> Cease your sin and dry your tears,
>   Jesus is always ready!'"

"And dretful lucky for you He is!" muttered Samantha, who had come to look for Timothy. "Jabe! Jabe! Has Timothy gone for the cow?"

"Dunno. Jest what I was goin' to ask you when I got roun' to it."

"Well, how are you goin' to find out?"

"Find out by seein' the cow if he hez gone, an' by not seein' no cow if he hain't. I'm comf'table either way it turns out. One o' them writin' fellers that was up here summerin'

Jabe singing

said, 'They also serve who'd ruther stan' 'n' wait''d be a good motto for me, 'n' he's about right when I've be'n hayin'. Look down there at the shiners, ain't they cool? Gorry! I wish I was a fish!"

"If you was you would n't wear your fins out, that's certain!"

"Come now, Samanthy, don't be hard on a feller after his day's work. Want me to git up 'n' blow the horn for the boy?"

"No, thank you," answered Samantha cuttingly. "I would n't ask you to blow out your precious breath for fear you 'd be too lazy to draw it in agin. When I want to get anything done I can gen'ally spunk up sprawl enough to do it myself, thanks be!"

"Wall now, Samanthy, you cheat the men-folks out of a heap o' pleasure bein' so all-fired independent, did ye know it?

"'Tremblin' sinner, calm your fears!
Jesus is always ready.'"

"When 'd you see him last?"

"I hain't seen him sence 'bout noon-time. Warn't he in to supper?"

"No. We thought he was off with you. Well, I guess he 's gone for the cow, but I should think he 'd be hungry. It 's kind o' queer."

Miss Vilda was seated at the open window in the kitchen, and Lady Gay was enthroned in her lap, sleepy, affectionate, tractable, adorable.

"How would you like to live here at the White Farm, deary?" asked Miss Vilda.

"Oh, yet. I yike to yive here if Timfy doin' to yive here too. I yike oo, I yike Samfy, I yike Dabe, I yike white tat 'n' white tow 'n' white bossy 'n' my boofely desses 'n' my boofely dolly 'n' er day hen 'n' I yikes evelybuddy!"

"But you'd stay here like a nice little girl if Timothy had to go away, would n't you?"

"No, I won't tay like nite ittle dirl if Timfy do 'way. If Timfy do 'way, I do too. I's Timfy's dirl."

"But you're too little to go away with Timothy."

"Ven I ky an' keam an' kick an' hold my bwef — I s'ow you how!"

"No, you need n't show me how," said Vilda hastily. "Who do you love best, deary, Samanthy or me?"

"I yuv Timfy bet. Lemme twy rit-man-poor-man-bedder-man-fief on your buckalins, pease."

"Then you 'll stay here and be my little girl, will you?"

"Yet, I tay here an' be Timfy's ittle dirl. Now oo p'ay by your own seff ittle while,

Mit Vildy, pease, coz I dot to det down an
find Samfy an' put my dolly to bed coz she's
defful seepy."

"It's half past eight," said Samantha
coming into the kitchen, "and Timothy ain't
nowheres to be found, and Jabe hain't seen
him sence noon-time."

"You need n't be scared for fear you 've
lost your bargain," remarked Miss Vilda sarcastically. "There ain't so many places open
to the boy that he'll turn his back on this
one, I guess!"

Yet, though the days of chiv-
alry were over, that was precisely
what Timothy Jessup had done.

"Wilkins' Woods" was a quiet
stretch of timber land that lay
along the banks of Pleasant
River; and though the natives,
for the most part, would never
have noticed if it had been paved
with asphalt and roofed in with
oil-cloth, it was, nevertheless,
the most tranquil bit of loveliness in all the country round.

For there the river twisted and turned and
sparkled in the sun, and "bent itself in grace-
ful courtesies of farewell" to the hills it was
leaving ; and kissed the velvet meadows that
stooped to drink from its brimming cup ; and

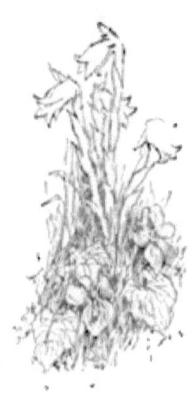

lapped the trees gently, as they
hung over its crystal mirrors the
better to see their own fresh beauty.
Here it wound "about and in and
out," laughing in the morning sunlight, to think of the tiny streamlet
out of which it grew ; paling and
shimmering at evening when it
held the stars and moonbeams in
its bosom ; and trembling in the
night wind to think of the great unknown
sea into whose arms it was hurrying.

Here was a quiet pool where the rushes
bent to the breeze and the quail dipped her
wing ; there, a winding path where the cattle
came down to the edge, and having looked
upon the scene and found it all very good,
dipped their sleek heads to drink and drink
and drink of the river's nectar. The first
pink mayflowers pushed their sweet heads
through the reluctant earth here, and there

waxen Indian pipes grew in the moist places, and yellow violets hid themselves beneath their modest leaves.

And here sat Timothy, with his heart in his eyes, bidding good-by to all this soft and tender loveliness; by his side, faithful unto death (but very much in hopes of something better), sat Rags, who thought it a fine enough prospect, but one that could be beaten at all points by a bit of shed-view he knew of, — a superincumbent hash-pan, an empty milk-dish, and an emaciated white cat flying round a corner! The remembrance of these past joys brought the tears to his eyes, but he forbore to let them flow lest he should add to the griefs of his little master, which, for aught he knew, might be as heavy as his own.

Timothy was comporting himself, at this trying crisis, neither as a hero nor as a martyr. There is no need of exaggerating his virtues. Enough to say, not that he was a hero, but that he had in him the stuff out of which heroes are made. Win his heart and fire his imagination, and there is no splendid deed of which the boy would not have been capable. That he knew precisely what he was leaving behind, or what he was going forth to meet, would be saying too much. One thing he did know : Miss Vilda had said distinctly that two was one too many, and that he was the objectionable unit referred to. In addition to this, he had more than once heard that nobody in Pleasant River wanted him, but there would be plenty of homes open to Gay if he were safely out of the way. A little allusion to a Home, which he caught when he was just bringing in a four-leaved clover to show to Samantha, completed the stock of ideas from which he reasoned. He was very clear on one point : that he would never be taken alive and put in a Home with a capital H. He respected Homes, he approved of them, for other boys, but personally they were unpleasant to him, and he had no intention of dwelling in one if he could help it. The situation did not appear utterly hopeless in his eyes. He had his original dollar and eighty-five cents in money ; Rags and he had supped like kings off wild blackberries and hard gingerbread ; and, more than all, he was young and merci-

fully blind to everything but the immediate
present. Yet, even in taking the most com-
monplace possible view of his character, it
would be folly to affirm that he was anything
but unhappy. His soul was not sustained
by the consciousness of having done a self-
forgetting and manly act; for he was not old
enough to have such a consciousness, which
is something the good God gives us a little
later on, to help us over some of the hard
places.

"Nobody wants me! Nobody wants me!"
he sighed, as he lay down under the trees.
"Nobody ever did want me, — I wonder
why! And everybody loves my darling Gay
and wants to keep her, and I don't wonder
about that. But oh, if I only belonged to
somebody! (Cuddle up close, little Ragsy;
we've got nobody but just each other, and
you can put your head into the other pocket
that has n't got the gingerbread in it, if you
please!) If I only was like that little
butcher's boy that he lets ride on the seat
with him, and hold the reins when he takes
meat into the houses, — or if I only was
that freckle-face boy with the straw hat that

lives on the way to the store! His mother
keeps coming out to the gate on purpose to
kiss him. Or if I was even Billy Pennell!
He's had three mothers and two fathers
in three years, Jabe says. Jabe likes me, I
think, but he can't have me live at his house,
because his mother is the kind that needs
plenty of room, he says, — and Samanthy
has no house. But I did what I tried to do.
I got away from Minerva Court and found a
lovely place for Gay to live, with two mothers
instead of one ; and maybe they 'll tell her
about me when she grows bigger, and then
she'll know I did n't want to run away from
her, but whether they tell her or not, she's
only a baby, and boys must always take care
of girls ; that 's what my dream-mother whis-
pers to me in the night — and that 's . . .
what . . . I 'm always . . ."

Come! gentle sleep, and take this friendless little knight-errant in thy kind arms!
Bear him across the rainbow bridge, and lull
him to rest with the soft plash of waves and
sighing of branches! Cover him with thy
mantle of dreams, sweet goddess, and give
him in sleep what he hath never had in
waking!

Meanwhile, a more dramatic scene was being enacted at the White Farm. It was nine o'clock, and Samantha had gone from pond to garden, shed to barn, and gate to dairy, a dozen times; but there was no sign of Timothy. Gay had refused to be undressed till "Timfy" appeared on the premises, but had fallen asleep in spite of the most valiant resolution, and was borne upstairs by Samantha, who made her ready for bed without waking her.

As she picked up the heap of clothes to lay them neatly on a chair, a bit of folded paper fell from the bosom of the little dress. She glanced at it, turned it over and over, read it quite through. Then, after retiring behind her apron a moment, she went swiftly downstairs to the dining-room where Miss Avilda and Jabe were sitting.

" There !" she exclaimed, with a triumphant sob, as she laid the paper down in front of the astonished couple. " That 's a letter from Timothy. He 's run away, 'n' I don't blame him a mite, 'n' I hope folks 'll be satisfied now they 've got red of the blessed angel, 'n' turned him ou'doors with-

out a roof to his head!   Read it out, 'n' see
what kind of a boy we 've showed the door
to!"

Dere Miss vilder and sermanthy.   i herd
you say i cood not stay here enny longer

The Letter

and other people sed
nobuddy wood have
me and what you sed
about the home but
as i do not like homes
i am going to run
away if its all the
same to you. Please
give Jabe back his
birds egs with my
love and i am sorry i broak the humming-
bird's one but it was a naxident.   Pleas take
good care of gay and i will come back and
get her when I am ritch.   I thank you very
mutch for such a happy time and the white
farm is the most butifull plase in the whole
whirld.   TIM.

   p. s. i wood not tell you if i was going to
stay but billy penel thros stones at the white
cow witch i fere will get into her milk so no
more from   TIM.

p. s. i am sorry not to say good by but i am afrade on acount of the home so i put them here.

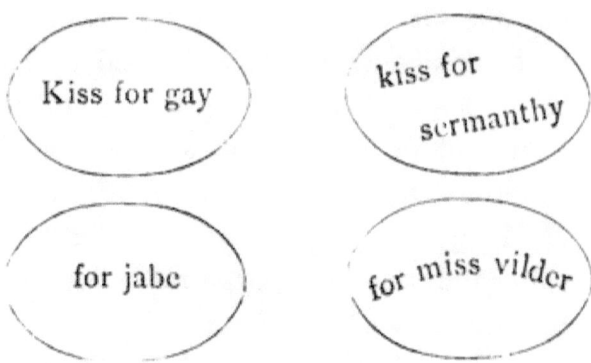

Kiss for gay

kiss for sermanthy

for jabe

for miss vilder

The paper fell from Miss Vilda's trembling fingers, and two salt tears dropped into the kissing places.

"The Lord forgive me!" she said at length, — it was many a year since any one had seen her so moved. "The Lord forgive me for a hard-hearted old woman, and give me a chance to make it right. Not one reproachful word does he say to us about showin' partiality, — not one! And my heart has kind of yearned over that boy from the first, but just because he had Marthy's eyes he kept bringin' up the past to me, and I never looked at him without re-

memberin' how hard and unforgivin' I'd
be'n to her, and thinkin' if I'd petted and
humored her a little and made life pleasanter,
perhaps she'd never have gone away. And
I've scrimped and saved and laid up money
till it comes hard to pay it out, and when
I thought of bringin' up and schoolin' two
children I cal'lated I could n't afford it ; and
yet I've got ten thousand dollars in the
bank and the best farm for miles around.
Samanthy, you go fetch my bonnet and

Melted

shawl, — Jabe, you go
and hitch up Maria,
and we'll go after
that boy and fetch
him back if he's to
be found anywheres
above ground ! And
if we come across
any more o' the
same family trampin'
around the country,

we'll bring them along home while we're
about it, and see if we can't get some sleep
and some comfort out o' life. The Missionary Society will have to look some-

wheres else for money, I guess. There's plenty o' folks that don't get good works set right down in their front yards for 'em to do. I 'll look out for the individyals for a spell, and let the other folks support the societies ! "

SCENE XV

WILKINS' WOODS

*Like all Dogs in Fiction, the Faithful Rags guides
Miss Vilda to his Little Master*

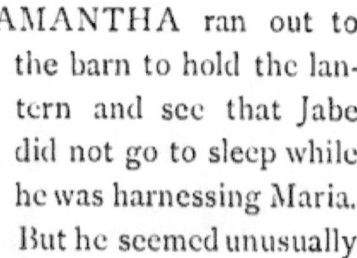

AMANTHA ran out to the barn to hold the lantern and see that Jabe did not go to sleep while he was harnessing Maria. But he seemed unusually "spry" for him, although he was conducting himself in a somewhat strange and unusual manner. His loose figure shook from time to time, as with severe chills; he appeared too weak to hold up the shafts, so he finally dropped them and hung round Maria's neck in a sort of mild speechless convulsion.

"What under the canopy ails you, Jabe Slocum?" asked Samantha. "I s'pose it's one o' them everlastin' old addled jokes o' yourn you're tryin' to hatch out, but it's a poor time to be jokin' now. What's the matter with you?"

"'Ask me no questions 'n' I'll you no lies' is an awful good motto," chuckled Jabe, with a new explosion of mirth that stretched his mouth to an alarming extent. "Oh, there, I can't hold in 'nother minute. I shall bust if I don' tell somebody! Set down on that nail kag, Samanthy, 'n' I 'll let you hev a leetle slice o' this joke — if you 'll keep it to yourself. You see I know — 'bout — whar — to look — for this here — runaway!"

"You hevn't got him stowed away anywheres, hev you? If you hev, it 'll be the last joke you 'll play on Vildy Cummins, I can tell you that much, Jabe Slocum."

"No, I hain't stowed him away, but I can tell putty nigh whar he 's stowed hisself away, and I 'm ready to die a-laffin' to see how it 's all turned out jest as I suspicioned 't would. You see, Samanthy Ann, I thought 'bout a week ago 't would be well enough to kind o' create a demand for the young ones so 't they 'd hev some kind of a market value, and so I got Elder Southwick 'n' Aunt Hitty kind o' started on that tack. It worked out slick as a whistle, for they did n't know I was usin' of 'em as innercent instruments, and Aunt Hitty don't need much encouragement to talk ; it 's a heap easier for her to drizzle 'n it is to hold up! Well, I 've be'n surmis-

in' for a week that the boy meant to run
away, and to-day I was dead sure of it; for
he come to me this afternoon, when I was
restin' a spell on account o' the hot sun, and
he was awful low-sperrited, 'n' he asked me
every namable kind of a question you ever
hearn tell of, and all so simple-minded that I
jest turned him inside out 'thout his knowin'
what I was doin'. Well, when I found out
what he was up to I could 'a' stopped him
then 'n' there, tho' I don' know 's I would
anyhow, for I should n't like livin' in a 'sylum
any better 'n he does; but thinks I to myself, thinks I, I 'd better let him run away,
jest as he 's a-plannin', — and why? Cause
it 'll show what kind o' stuff he 's made of,
and that he ain't no beggar layin' roun' whar
he ain't wanted, but a self-respectin' boy
that 's wuth lookin' after. And thinks I,
Samanthy 'n' I know the wuth of him
a'ready, but there 's them that hain't waked
up to it yit, namely, Miss Vildy Trypheny
Cummins; and as Miss Vildy Trypheny
Cummins is that kind o' cattle that can't be
drove, but hez to be kind o' coaxed along,
mebbe this runnin'-away bizness 'll be the

thing that 'll fetch her roun' to our way o' thinkin'. Now I would n't deceive nobody for a farm down East with a pig on it, but thinks I, there ain't no deceivin' 'bout this. He don' know I know he 's goin' to run away, so he 's all square; and he never told me nothin' 'bout his plans, so I 'm all square; and Miss Vildy 's good as eighteen-karat gold when she gets roun' to it, so she 'll be all square; and Samanthy 's got her blinders on 'n' don't see nothin' to the right nor to the left, so she 's all square. And I ain't interferin' with nobody. I 'm jest lettin' things go the way they 've started, 'n' stan'in' to one side to see whar they 'll fetch up, kind o' like Providence. I 'm leavin' Miss Vildy a free agent, but I 'm shapin' circumstances so 's to give her a chance. But land! if I 'd fixed up the thing to suit myself I could n't 'a' managed it as Timothy hez, 'thout knowin' that he was managin' anything. Look at that letter bizness now! I could n't 'a' writ that letter better myself! And the sperrit o' the little feller, jest takin' his dorg 'n' lightin' out with nothin' but a perlite goodby! Well I can't stop to talk no more 'bout it now, or we won't ketch him, but we 'll jest try Wilkins' Woods, Maria, 'n' see how that goes. The river road leads to Edgewood 'n' Hillside, whar there 's consid'able hayin' bein' done, as I happened to mention to Timothy this afternoon ; and plenty o' black-berries 'side the road, 'specially after you pass the wood-pile on the left-hand side, whar there 's a reg'lar garding of 'em right 'side of an old hoss-blanket that 's layin' there ; one that I happened to leave there one time when I was sleepin' ou'doors for my health, and that was this afternoon 'bout five o'clock, so I guess it hain't changed its location sence."

Jabe and Miss Vilda drove in silence along the river road that skirted Wilkins' Woods, a place where Jabe had taken Tim-othy more than once, so he informed Miss Vilda, and a likely road for him to travel if he were on his way to some of the near vil-lages.

Poor Miss Vilda! Fifty years old, and in twenty summers and winters scarcely one lovely thought had blossomed into lovelier deed and shed its sweetness over her arid

Transformed

and colorless life. Now, under the magic spell of tender little hands and innocent lips, of luminous eyes that looked wistfully into hers for a welcome and the touch of a groping helplessness that fastened upon her strength, the woman in her woke into life, and the beauty and fragrance of long-ago summers came back again as in a dream.

After having driven three or four miles, they heard a melancholy sound in the distance; and as they approached a huge woodpile on the left side of the road, they saw a small woolly form perched on a little rise of ground, howling most melodiously at the August moon, that hung like a ball of red fire in the cloudless sky.

"That's a sign of death in the family, ain't it, Jabe?" whispered Miss Vilda faintly.

Howling at the Moon

"So they say," he answered cheerfully; "but if 't is, I can 'count for it, bein' as how I fertilized the pond lilies with a mess o' four white kittens this afternoon; and as Rags was with me when I done it, he may know what he 's bayin' 'bout, — if 't is Rags, 'n' it looks enough like him to be him, — 'n' it is him, by Jiminy, 'n' Timothy 's sure to be somewheres near. I 'll get out 'n' look roun' a little."

"You set right still, Jabe; I 'll get out myself, for if I find that boy I 've got something to say to him that nobody can say for me."

He knew Maria

As Jabe drew the wagon up beside the fence, Rags bounded out to meet them. He knew Maria, bless your soul, the minute he clapped his eyes on her, and as he approached Miss Vilda's congress boot his quivering whiskers seemed to say, "Now, where have I smelled that boot before? If I mistake not, it has been applied to me more than once. Ha! I have it! Miss Vilda Cummins of the White Farm, owner of the white cat and hash-pan, and companion of the lady with the firm hand, who wields the broom !" whereupon he leaped up on Miss Cummins' black alpaca skirts, and made for her flannel garters in a way that she particularly disliked.

"Now," said she, "if he's anything like the dogs you hear tell of, he'll take us right to Timothy."

"Wall, I don' know," said Jabe cautiously ; "there's so many kinds o' dorg in him you can't hardly tell what he will do. When dorgs is mixed beyond a certain p'int it kind o' muddles up their instincks, 'n' you can't rely on 'em. Still, you might try him. Hold still, 'n' see what he'll do."

Miss Vilda "held still," and Rags jumped on her skirts.

"Now, set down, 'n' see whar he'll go."

Miss Vilda sat down, and Rags went into her lap.

"Now, make believe start somewheres, 'n' mebbe he'll get ahead 'n' put you on the right track."

Miss Vilda did as she was told, and Rags followed close at her heels.

"Gorry ! I never see sech a fool !— or

wait, -- I 'll tell you what 's the matter with him. Mebbe he ain't sech a fool as he looks. You see, he knows Timothy wants to run away and don't want to be found 'n' clapped into a 'sylum, 'n' nuther does he. And not bein' sure o' your intentions, he ain't a-goin' to give hisself away; that 's the way I size Mr. Rags up !"

"Nice doggy, nice doggy !" shuddered Miss Vilda, as Rags precipitated himself upon her again. "Show me where Timothy is, and then we 'll go back home and have some nice bones. Run and find your little master, that 's a good doggy !"

It would be a clever philosopher who could divine Rags' special method of logic, or who could write him down either as fool or sage. Suffice it to say that, at this moment, having run in all other possible directions, and wishing, doubtless, to keep on moving, he ran round the wood-pile; and Miss Vilda, following close behind, came upon a little figure stretched on a bit of gray blanket. The pale face shone paler in the moonlight; there were traces of tears on the cheeks; but there was a heavenly smile on his parted lips, as if his dream-mother had rocked him to sleep in her arms. Rags stole away to Jabe (for even mixed dogs have some delicacy), and Miss Vilda went down on her knees beside the sleeping boy.

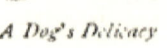

"Timothy, Timothy, wake up!"

No answer.

"Timothy, wake up! I 've come to take you home!"

Timothy woke with a sob and a start at that hated word, and seeing Miss Vilda at once jumped to conclusions.

A Dog's Delicacy

"Please, please, dear Miss Vildy, don't take me to the Home, but find me some other place, and I 'll never, never run away from it!"

"You blessed child, I 've come to take you back to your own home at the White Farm."

It was too good to believe all at once.

"Nobody wants me there," he said hesitatingly.

"Everybody wants you there," replied Miss Vilda, with a softer note in her voice than anybody had ever heard there before.

"Samantha wants you, Gay wants you, and Jabe is waiting out here with Maria, for he wants you."

"But it's your house and you don't want me!" faltered the boy.

"I want you more than all of 'em put together Timothy; I want you, and I need you most of all," cried Miss Vilda, with the

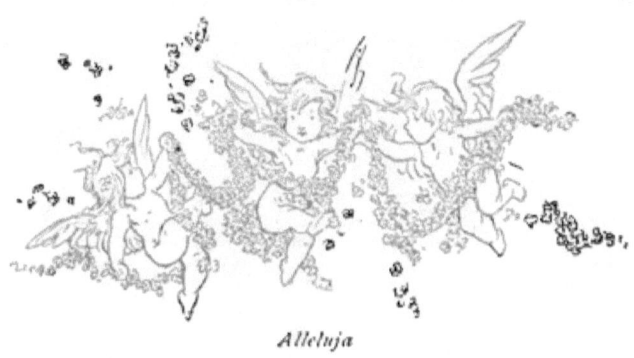

Alleluja

tears coursing down her withered cheeks; "if you'll only forgive me for hurtin' your feelin's and makin' you run away, you shall come to the White Farm and be my own boy as long as you live."

"Oh, Miss Vildy, darling Miss Vildy! are we both of us adopted, and are we truly going to live with you all the time and never have to go to the Home?" Whereupon,

the boy flung his loving arms round Miss
Vilda's neck in an ecstasy of gratitude;
and in that sweet embrace of trust and
confidence and joy, the stone was rolled
away, once and forever, from the sepulchre
of Miss Vilda's heart, and Easter morning
broke there.

SCENE XVI

THE NEW HOMESTEAD

*Timothy's Quest is ended, and Samanthy says,
" Come along, Dave ! "*

J ABE SLOCUM! Do you know it's goin' on seven o'clock 'n' not a single chore done?"

Jabe yawned, turned over, and listened to Samantha's unwelcome voice, which (considerably louder than the voice of conscience) came from the outside world to disturb his delicious morning slumbers.

"Jabe Slocum I say! Do you hear me?"

"Hear you? Gorry! you'd wake the seven sleepers if they was anywhar within ear-shot!"

"Wal, will you git up?"

"Yes, I'll git up if you're goin' to hev a brash 'bout it, but I wish you hed n't waked me so awful suddent. 'Don't ontwist the mornin' glory''s my motto. Wait a spell 'n' the sun 'll do it, 'n' save a heap o' wear 'n' tear besides. Go 'long! I 'll git up."

"I 've heerd that story afore, 'n' I won't go 'long tell I hear you step foot on the floor."

"Scoot! I tell yer I 'll be out in a jiffy."

"Yes, I think I see yer. Your jiffies are consid'able like golden opportunities, there ain't time for more 'n one of 'em in a lifetime!" and having shot this Parthian arrow, Samantha departed as one having done her duty in that humble sphere of action to which it had pleased Providence to call her.

These were beautiful autumn days at the White Farm. The orchards were gleaming, the grapes hung purple on the vines, and the odor of ripening fruit was in the hazy air. The pink spirea had cast its feathery petal by the gray stone walls, but the welcome goldenrod bloomed in royal profusion along the brown waysides, and a crimson leaf hung here and there in the treetops, just to give a hint of the fall styles in color. Heaps of yellow pumpkins and squashes lay in the corners of the fields; cornstalks bowed their heads beneath the weight of ripened ears; beans threatened to burst through their yellow pods; the sound of the threshing-machine was heard in the land; and the "hull univarse wanted to be waited on to once," according to Jabe Slocum; for, as he affirmed, "Yer couldn't ketch up with your work nohow, for if yer set up nights 'n' worked Sundays, the craps 'd ripen 'n' go to seed on yer 'fore yer could git 'em harvested!"

If there was peace and plenty without, there was quite as much within doors.

"I can't hardly tell what 's the matter with me these days," said Samantha Ann to Miss Vilda, as they sat peeling and slicing apples for drying. "My heart has felt like a stun these last years, and now all to once it 's so soft I 'm ashamed of it. Seems to me there never was such a summer! The hay never smelt so sweet, the birds never sang so well, the currants never jelled so hard! Why I

can't kick the cat, though she's more everlastin'ly under foot 'n ever, 'n' pretty soon I
shan't even have sprawl enough to jaw Jabe
Slocum.   I b'lieve it's nothin' in the world

Going to see the Chickens

but them children !
They keep a-runnin'
after me, 'n' it's dear
Samanthy here, 'n' dear
Samanthy there, jest
as if I warn't a hombly
old maid ; 'n' they take
holt o' my hands on
both sides o' me, 'n'
won't stir a step till I
go to see the chickens
with 'em, 'n' the pig, 'n'
one thing 'n' 'nother,
'n' clappin' their hands
when I make 'em gin-
ger-bread men, and kissin' of me when I give
'em pond lilies to smell of.   And that reminds
me, I see the school-teacher goin' down along
this mornin', 'n' I run out to see how Timothy
was gittin' along in his studies.   She says he's
the most ex-tra-ordinary scholar in this dees-
trick.   She says he takes holt of every book

she gives him jest as if 't was reviewin' 'stid o'
the first time over. She says when he speaks
pieces, Friday afternoons, all the rest o' the
young ones set there with their jaws hangin',
'n' some of 'em laughin' 'n' cryin' 't the same
time. She says we'd oughter see some of
his comp'sitions 'n' she'll show us some as
soon as she gits 'em back from her beau
that works at the Waterbury Watch Factory,
and they're goin' to be married 's quick as
she gits money enough saved up to buy her
weddin' clo'es, 'n' I told her not to put it off
too long or she'd hev her clo'es on her hands,
'stid of her back. She
says Timothy's at the
head of the hull class,
but land! there ain't
a boy in it that knows
enough to git his
clo'es on right side
out. She's a splen-
did teacher, Miss
Boothby is! She

The Young Poet

tells me the seeleck men hev raised her pay
to four dollars a week 'n' she to board herself, 'n' she's wuth every cent of it. I like

to see folks well paid that 's got the patience to set indoors 'n' cram information inter young ones that don't care no more 'bout learnin' 'n' a skunk-blackbird. She give me Timothy's writin' book for you to see what he writ in it yesterday, 'n' she hed to keep him in 't recess 'cause he did n't copy 'Go to the ant, thou sluggard, and be wise,' as he 'd oughter. Now let 's see what 't is. My grief! it 's poetry sure 's you 're born. I can tell it in a minute 'cause it don't come out to the aidge o' the book one side or the other. Read it out loud, Vildy."

"'Oh! the White Farm and the White Farm!
    I love it with all my heart;
And I 'm to live at the White Farm
    Till death it do us part.'"

Miss Vilda lifted her head, intoxicated with the melody she had evoked. "Did you ever hear anything like that," she exclaimed proudly.

"'Oh! the White Farm and the White Farm!
    I love it with all my heart;
And I 'm to live at the White Farm
    Till death it do us part.'"

"Just hear the sent'ment of it, and the way it sings along like a tune. I 'm goin' to

show that to the minister this very night,
and that boy's got to have the best education there is to be had if we have to mort-
gage the farm."

Samantha Ann was right. The old homestead wore a new aspect these days, and a
love of all things seemed to have crept into
the hearts of its inmates, as if some beneficent fairy of a spider were spinning a web
of tenderness all about the house, or as if a
soft light had dawned in the midst of great
darkness and was gradually brightening into
the perfect day.

In the midst of this new-found gladness
and the sweet cares that grew and multiplied
as the busy days went on, Samantha's appetite for happiness grew by what it fed upon,
so that before long she was a little unhappy
that other people, some more than others,
were not as happy as she ; and Aunt Hitty
was heard to say at the sewing-circle (which
had facilities for gathering and disseminat-
ing news infinitely superior to those of the
Associated Press), that Samantha Ann Ripley looked so peart and young this summer,
Dave Milliken had better spunk up and try
again.

But, alas! the younger and fresher and happier Samantha looked, the older and sadder and meeker David appeared, till all hopes of his "spunking up" died out of the village heart ; and, it might as well be stated, out of Samantha's also.   She always thought about it at sundown, for it was at sundown that all their quarrels and reconciliations had taken place, inasmuch as it was the only leisure time for week-day courting at Pleasant River.

It was sundown now ; Miss Vilda and Jabez Slocum had gone to Wednesday evening prayer-meeting, and Samantha was looking for Timothy to go to the store with her on some household errands.   She had seen the children go into the garden a half hour before, Timothy walking gravely, with his book behind him, Gay blowing over the grass like a feather.

She walked towards the summer-house ; Timothy was not there, but little Lady Gay was having a party all to herself, and the scene was such a pretty one that Samantha stooped behind the lattice and listened.

There was a table spread for four, with

bits of broken china and shells for dishes, and pieces of apple and gingerbread for the feast. There were several dolls present, notably one without any head, who was not likely to shine at a dinner party; but Gay's first-born sat in her lap. Only a mother could have gazed upon such a battered thing

The Dinner Party

and loved it. Gay took her pleasures madly, and this faithful creature had shared them all; but not having inherited her mother's somewhat rare recuperative powers, she was now fit only for a free bed in a hospital, — a state of mind and body which she did not in the least endeavor to conceal. One of her shoe-button eyes dangled by a linen thread in a blood-curdling sort of way. Her nose, which had been a pink glass bead, was now a mere spot, ambiguously located. Her red worsted lips were sadly raveled, but that she did not regret, "for it was kissin' as done it." Her yarn hair was attached to her head with safety-pins, and her internal organs intruded themselves on the public through a gaping wound in the side. Never mind! if you have any curiosity to measure the strength of the ideal, watch a child with her oldest doll. Rags sat at the head of the dinner-table, and had taken the precaution to get the headless doll on his right, with a view to eating her gingerbread as well as his own, — doing no violence to the proprieties in this way, but rather concealing her defects from a carping public.

"I tell you sompfin', ittle Mit Vildy Tummins," Gay was saying to her battered off-spring. "You's doin' to have a new ittle sit-ter to-mowowday, if you's a dood ittle dirl an does to seep nite an kick, you *sctweet* ittle Vildy Tummins!" (All this punctu-ated with ardent squeezes fraught with deli-cious agony to one who had a wound in her side!) "Vay fink you's worn out, 'weety, but we know you is n't, don' we, 'weety? An' I'll tell you nite ittle tory to-night, tause you is n't seepy. Wunt there was a ittle day hen 'at tole a net an' laid fir-teen waw edds in it, an' bime bye erleven or seventeen ittle chits f'ew out of 'em, an' Mit Vildy 'dopted 'em all! I'n't that a nite tory you *ser-weet* ittle Mit Vildy Tummins?"

Samantha hardly knew why the tears should spring to her eyes as she watched the dinner party, — unless it was because we can scarcely look at children in their unconscious play without a sort of sadness, partly of pity and partly of envy, and of longing too, as for something lost and gone. And Samantha could look back to the time when she had sat at tables set with bits of broken china, yes, in this very summer-house, and little Martha was always so gay, and David used to laugh so! "But there was no use in tryin' to make folks any dif'rent, 'specially if they was such nat'ral born fools they could n't see a hole in a grindstun 'thout hevin' it hung on their noses!" and with these large and charitable views of human nature, Samantha walked back to the gate, and met Timothy as he came out of the orchard. She knew then what he had been doing. The boy had certain quaint thoughts and ways that were at once a revelation and an inspiration to these two plain women, and one of them was to step softly into the side orchard on pleasant evenings, and without a word, to lay a nosegay on Martha's little white doorplate. If Miss Vilda chanced

to be at the window he would give her a quiet smile, much as to say, "We have no need of words, we two!" And Vilda, like one of old, hid all these doings in her heart of hearts, and loved the boy with a love passing knowledge.

Timothy's Thoughtfu'ness

Samantha, with Timothy by her side, walked down the hill to the store. Yes, David Milliken was sitting all alone on the loafer's bench at the door, and why was n't he at prayer-meetin,' where he ought to be?

She was glad she chanced to have on her clean purple calico, and that Timothy had insisted on pinning a pink Ma'thy Washington geranium in her collar, for it was just as well to make folks' mouth water whether they had sense enough to eat or not.

"Who is that sorry-looking man that always sits on the bench at the store, Samanthy?"

"That's David Milliken."

"Why does he look so sorry, Samanthy?"

"Oh, he's all right. He likes it fust-rate, wearin' out that hard bench settin' on it night in 'n' night out, like a bump on a log! But, there, Timothy, I 've gone 'n' forgot the whole pepper, 'n' we 're goin' to pickle seed cowcumbers to-morrer. You take the lard home 'n' put it in the cold room, 'n' ondress Gay 'n' git her to bed, for I 've got to call int' Mis Mayhew's goin' along back."

It was very vexatious to be obliged to pass David Milliken a second time; "though there warn't no sign that he cared anything about it one way or 'nother, bein' blind as a bat, 'n' deef as an adder, 'n' dumb as a fish,

'n' settin stockstill there with no coat on,
'n' the wind blowin' up for rain, 'n' four o'
the Millikens layin' in the churchyard with
gallopin' consumption." It was in this
frame of mind that she purchased the pepper, which she could have eaten at that
moment as calmly as if it had been marrow-
fat peas; and in this frame of mind she
might have continued to the end of time had
it not been for one of those unconsidered
trifles that move the world when the great
forces have given up trying. As she came
out of the store and passed David, her eye
fell on a patch in the flannel shirt that covered his bent shoulders. The shirt was gray
and (oh, the pity of it!) the patch was red;
moreover, it was laid forlornly on outside,
and held by straggling stitches of carpet
thread put in by patient, clumsy fingers.
That patch had an irresistible pathos for a
woman!

Samantha Ann Ripley never exactly knew
what happened. Even the wisest of New
England virgins has emotional lapses once
in a while, and this one confessed afterwards
that her heart riz right up inside of her like

a yeast cake. Mr. Berry, the postmaster,
was in the back of the store reading postal
cards. Not a soul was in sight. She managed to get down over the steps, though
something with the strength of tarred ship-
ropes was drawing her back ; and then, looking over her shoulder with her whole brave,
womanly heart in her swimming eyes, she
put out her hand and said, " Come along,
Dave ! "

And David straightway gat him up from
the loafer's bench and went unto Samantha
gladly.

And they remembered not past unhappi-
ness because of present joy ; nor that the
chill of coming winter was in the air, because it was summer in their hearts ; and
this is the eternal magic of love.